The Night Watchmen

The
Night Watchmen

by
HELEN CRESSWELL

illustrated by
GARETH FLOYD

ALADDIN BOOKS
MACMILLAN PUBLISHING COMPANY   NEW YORK

First published in Great Britain by Faber and Faber Limited.
Aladdin Books
Macmillan Publishing Company
866 Third Avenue, New York, NY 10022
First Aladdin Books edition 1989
Printed in United States of America

10 9 8 7 6 5 4 3 2 1

Library of Congress Cataloging-in-Publication Data
Cresswell, Helen.
The night watchmen/Helen Cresswell: illustrated by Gareth
Floyd.
    p.   cm.
Summary: Looking for something to fill his lonely days, a young
boy recuperating from a long illness meets two tramps who live in a
world that hardly seems real.
[1. Fantasy.]   I. Floyd, Gareth, 1940-   ill. II. Title. PZ7.C8645Ni
1989
[Fic]—dc19   88-29188   CIP   AC
ISBN 0-689-71292-8

For Osyth Leeston

Chapter 1

$\mathcal{H}$enry watched the diamond-shaped reflection from the mirror traveling slowly across the bedroom wall. This morning it seemed in even less of a hurry than usual. He didn't watch it all the time. If he did that, he felt sure it wouldn't move at all. Instead, he pretended to read, and every now and then took a quick glance over the top of the page. It had passed the second bunch of daisies on the wallpaper. There were two more bunches to go, and then the yellow flake of light would reach the gold-edged picture of "Storm at Sea" that Aunt Edith had given him last birthday.

"When it reaches the middle, the absolute middle," he told himself, "he'll come."

The book he was half reading became suddenly interesting, and next time he looked up he thought for one panicky moment that the reflection had gone. But it was still there, perched astride the gilt-edged frame, camouflaged, playing tricks on him.

He sat right up in bed and shook all his pillows.

Then he reached for his hairbrush and brushed first his hair and then his cheeks. The bristles scratched and his skin began to burn faintly.

"No remarks about roses in my cheeks *today*," he thought with satisfaction.

By the time he had cleared the comforter of books and puzzles the gold diamond was exactly in the middle of the picture, as if the sun had suddenly come out in that stormy sky. Henry frowned. The doctor should be here. He was a punctual man.

"I am a punctual man," he often said to Henry's mother. He had a gold watch on a long chain and would snap it shut as he spoke.

"He's not coming," Henry thought. "It's past his time."

The imprisoned yellow sun was edging toward the golden bar of the frame.

"Unless someone has broken a leg. That would make him late."

He lay there, every now and then scrubbing his cheeks.

"*Two* people must have broken their legs," he thought as the golden spot went over the edge of the picture and was free among the daisies again. "Or one person has broken both legs. Or a leg and an arm. Or two arms."

Henry let out a sigh so long and vast that he did not hear the doctor's car draw up. He heard the bell chime in the hall, though, and hastily gave his cheeks a last brush as he heard them coming up the stairs.

"And how's the little patient today?" asked the doctor, as he always did. He looked hard at Henry. "A little flushed, don't you think, Mother? Let me just pop this in."

A cold thin thermometer slid under his tongue. The doctor held his wrist in his own big hands.

"Hmmm. That's all right. Right as rain. Doing very nicely, Mrs. Crane."

"What about getting up?" Henry's voice was cracked. He cleared his throat. "You said that today you'd see about it."

"So I did. I did. Hmmm." He took out his watch, looked at it and clicked it shut, as if looking at the time would help him make up his mind. "Right. You can get up."

Henry fell back on his pillows, overjoyed. He hardly heard what the doctor was saying to his mother: "Just a few hours each day at first. . . . Plenty of fresh air . . . well wrapped up . . . build him up . . . at least a month. . . ."

He had been in bed for nearly a month. At first he had not minded. He had hardly even realized, as he tossed and threshed, wrestling dragons with fiery tongues. His world had shrunk to the four walls of his room. Even downstairs had become very far away and mysterious, with its muffled sounds of dishes clattering and music playing and voices in the hall.

As soon as the doctor had gone Henry got up. He felt as if his legs might fold under him at any minute, like a deck chair. The next day he felt stronger, and the next. On the fourth day he went out into the garden. It was March, all daffodil sun and racing clouds.

"I'm better!" he thought jubilantly as he ran down the lawn toward the fields beyond. "And I've got three weeks' holiday—nearly a month, in fact."

So splendid did the prospect seem that he made up his mind there and then to be as ill as possible every year. The days ahead seemed so brimful with possibilities that he hardly knew where to begin. He went tadpoling in the fast-running dike at the end of the orchard. A row of jam jars filled his bedroom mantelpiece. He flew his kite and made a new catapult. He built a dam. He made a raft.

Then suddenly he was bored. He realized for the first time that his holiday would be spent alone. All his friends were at school. They yelled and clattered past every morning while he still lay in bed, and then the streets were silent again. Three long weeks stretched ahead of him, empty and gray as the asphalt pavement itself.

Henry decided to go to the park, and for the first time ventured outside into the street. All the gates were closed, the curtains neatly drawn back. He saw the milkman, and that was all.

The park was deserted. He wandered gloomily through the wrought-iron gates and made for the aviary, where he glowered ferociously at the golden-eyed tropical birds. Picking up a stick, he ran it noisily over the bars of the cages. They flew in a rainbow whirl of feathers, squawking their protest.

The cockatoos bristled and threw out angry ruffs.

Henry sauntered off toward the swings. He passed a gardener putting in bedding plants.

"Good morning," he said.

"Morning." The man did not even lift his head. He knelt hunchbacked over his boxes, deaf and self-contained as a tortoise.

Henry went right to the farthest side of the park, where narrow paths twisted among the shrubbery. He had given up hope. And then he rounded a sudden corner, looked up, and saw the tramp. Sun struck the dew that glinted on his hair and beard. Wild, wicked and impossible he loomed among the clipped, self-respecting laurels.

"Good gracious!" said Henry.

"Good morning," said the tramp. "Nice day. Lovely. *Glorious*."

"Very nice," agreed Henry, delighted to be in conversation with someone at last, especially with a tramp of whom his mother would certainly have disapproved. He was folding newspapers with his mittened fingers.

"Making me bed," he explained. "Least, packing it up. Can't let this lot go. Nothing like *The Times* for warmth, and not so easy to come by every day of the week."

"You've been sleeping rolled up in newspapers!" said Henry, enchanted. "Are they really warm?"

"Downright frostproof," said the tramp. "Though sacks is good. Fair to middling, sacks."

He had finished stacking his newspapers and put

them into the wooden handbarrow parked by the seat.

"Seen any keepers?" he inquired.

"Only a gardener," said Henry, "and I think he was deaf. Don't they let you sleep here, then?"

"Not if they can help it," the tramp replied, "but they can't help it, mostly. I just nip among the bushes till they shut the big gates for the night. Worst thing is if they find you in the morning, first thing. Nasty shock that. Very nasty. I don't go in much for park sleeping. You've not seen Caleb, 'ave you?"

"Caleb?" said Henry.

"Brother," explained the tramp. "He's Caleb and I'm Josh. We split up, see, when we're park sleeping. Safer."

He burrowed into the handcart and fetched out a parcel. He unwrapped it and laid it on his knee. There were thick cheese sandwiches and an apple.

"Breakfast," he said thickly, his cheeks bulging.

Henry stared at him as he ate. Dew dangled from the rim of his battered felt hat. The edges of his overcoat were frayed almost to fringes, and it was tied round the middle with a rope. His boots were huge and craggy, and pieces of sack were tied round his legs like gaiters. It could not have been his clothes that made Henry think, for a moment, of a parson. It was his whiskers, he decided, gray and overgrown. Or it was the wild tufts of eyebrows, or his voice, rich and with built-in echoes as if it were in church.

Abruptly he stuffed the empty bag in his pocket, got up, and began to stamp. His arms flapped across his chest and he roared with the gusto of a furnace bellows.

"Ah! That's better! Get the blood bouncing. Stamp your feet and clap your wings. 'Ello, 'ere's Caleb."

Caleb was pushing his handbarrow toward them between the dripping laurels. The sun flashed on his fiery hair and beard. He was small and neat as a weasel, lard-faced and slippery-looking.

"Not so drafty here as where I been," he remarked, dropping the handles of his barrow. "The wind fair whistles round that statcher of Boadicea. Every last paper in my barrow I had to use. Who's this?"

He stared at Henry.

"Young feller," explained Josh, "by the name of . . . ?"

"Henry," said Henry.

"What does he want?" asked Caleb.

Josh shook his head.

"What do you want?" he asked Henry.

"Nothing," replied Henry.

"That's all right, then," said Caleb. "As long as he don't want anything, he won't be surprised to get nothing. You had your breakfast, Josh?"

He nodded.

"And packed up? Ready to go ticking?"

"Don't be in such a hurry, Caleb," Josh told him. "That's your main trouble. Always of a rush and tumble. Steady up a bit, like I do."

"If we went as steady as *you'd* like," said Caleb, "we should be statchers, more or less. Grass could grow under your feet, Josh, and that's a fact."

"Everywhere you been, *I* been," said Josh with dignity. "And that's just about practically everywhere. That don't sound like any statcher that *I* know of."

"We've got this whole town to get the ticking of before dark," said Caleb. He lowered his voice. "Either ways, go or stay, it'll mean the night train!"

"That's all right," replied Josh easily. "I can feel the ticking of this town right this minute. I've seen a flight of pigeons, and that I like. I've had a quiet night, and no keepers, and that I like. And I've met this young feller here, and *that* I like."

"You're too easy taken in, Josh," said Caleb impatiently. "The minute you see a bit o' sun shining you let all sense go. Flight of pigeons!"

"It's a sign," said Josh. He was tying a sack round his waist like an apron, very deft and housewifely. "Pigeons has always been a sign with me. I tell you this town ticks as sweet as ever I've heard."

Henry was smothering with mystification.

"What's ticking, Mr. Josh?" he asked, not because he thought it a wise thing to do, in view of Caleb's suspicious nature and red beard, but because with all these remarks about tickings and night trains, the choice was between asking and bursting.

Josh opened his mouth to reply.

"Don't tell him!" cried Caleb, quick as lightning.

Josh closed his mouth. In the silence the dew dropped heavily and the blanketed roar of traffic came up from the town below. Both the tramps were looking at Henry. Neither of them said a word. He supposed that he was the one who was meant to speak next.

"I didn't mean to be rude," he said at last. "I just wanted——"

"Just nothing!" snapped Caleb. He was all atwitch and aquiver now, foxier than ever.

"Now then, Caleb," protested Josh, "he meant no harm. He only——"

"*You* know the rules of this game, Josh," snapped Caleb. "If there's no questions allowed, there's no answers asked for. And you know as well as I do that children is the worst possible for asking questions. Ask, ask, ask, from morning till night. *You* know how they pester."

"But they're on our side," pointed out Josh. "They're natural, born, do-as-you-pleasers—leastways, till they're twelve or thereabouts."

Caleb seized the handles of his barrow.

"I'm off," he said. "I'm off ticking. And there's bridges to be looked over. Give an inch, and you lose a mile."

He set off down the wet path with a vicious squeaking of wheels. Josh looked regretfully at Henry.

"Sorry, young feller," was all he said. Then he, too, was off, with a slow duck-footed tread.

Henry was left looking after them with a curious feeling of being left on the other side of some invisible fence, and an equally certain feeling that the best place on earth to be would be on *their* side.

Chapter 2

$\mathcal{H}$enry spent much of the rest of the day wondering why he had not followed the pair while he had the chance. He had just stood there till they rounded the bend out of sight, then gone in the other direction, kicking at loose stones and so deep in speculation about the two tramps that it was only when it was much, much too late that he had decided he must see them again or die of curiosity.

He had never met a tramp before—not to speak to—but was nonetheless quite certain that Josh and Caleb were no ordinary run-of-the-mill vagrants. Quite apart from the mysterious allusions to "ticking" and "night trains," they had had a certain quivering aliveness, a sort of larger-than-lifeness, that was more like certain characters he had read about in books than people he had actually met in real life. The more Henry pondered on them, the more he knew that the pair were quite extraordinarily extraordinary.

He decided that they must still be somewhere

about the town, engaged in the mysterious pursuit of "ticking." He therefore set himself the task of finding them. He went straight down toward the town with the anxious feeling that if they were to be found, it must be during the remaining hours of daylight. The words "night train" ran like a refrain through the search of Mandover that now began.

He spent the whole morning combing the streets and went at last grudgingly home for lunch, knowing that he would be made to lie down for an hour afterward, as usual. He was. He lay there fuming at the delay while his thoughts turned again to the morning's encounter and he went over and over it, trying to remember every word for some vital clue that he might have missed.

When he woke it was past four o'clock. He sprang up and stared incredulously at his watch. He had been asleep! He had wasted the whole afternoon. He made for the door, only to stop even as he reached it. It was no use. Tea was at half-past four. By the time it was over, there would be only an hour of daylight left. It was too late.

All the same Henry left the house at half-past five and made his way down toward the town again. When he reached the market square, lights were beginning to shaft into the dusk and people were hurrying toward home. Henry stood for a minute or two, just staring at the pigeons that walked, nodding, over the paved square. Josh had said that pigeons were a "sign." To Henry they were no sign at all.

"If only I were a dog!" he thought desperately. If only he had some kind of a scent to follow through the narrow, milling streets. Without really thinking, he turned off one of the side roads and within a few minutes was walking down the deserted badly lit road that ran along the side of the canal. On one side reared the dark faceless walls of warehouses, on the other the canal ran, all smooth black and silver. Beyond the water were warehouses again. It was the blankest road in England.

Ahead of him Henry could see the arches of the bridge that spanned the road and water in three strides, and even that reminded him of the tramps. What was it Caleb had said—"There's bridges to be looked over. . . ." At that moment a train went over. There was a shuddering roar, a glimpse of lighted carriages and it was gone, leaving a vast, roaring echo under the arches that slowly ebbed into silence. For the first time Henry noticed his own footsteps.

"At least they couldn't have been on that train," he thought. "It was going too fast." The station was less than half a mile away. It must have been a through train. Nor, oddly, could he even begin to picture Josh and Caleb boarding a train at all. He tried to imagine them in the station, buying their tickets, putting a dime in a slot for chocolate, consulting the timetable. He failed. In any case, what about their barrows?

Henry stopped short. If they *had* gone ("go or stay, it means a night train") where had they left their barrows? Not checked at the station, of that he felt sure. Not with friends—they were strangers to the town. Somewhere safe, somewhere hidden, somewhere . . .

All in a moment Henry was certain he knew the answer. He turned and sped back the way he had come, his ears filled with the thunder of his own footsteps. In the market square he jumped on a bus that was just pulling out, and five minutes later was standing outside the high wrought-iron gates of the park. They were locked. Beyond them Henry could see the faint streak that was the path leading to the aviaries and ornamental gardens.

On either side of the ten-foot iron gates were low, spiky railings mounted on a stone wall. Henry looked swiftly about him, then nimbly stepped up on to the stone, swung his legs over the railings one at a time, and next minute was pushing his way triumphantly through the shrubbery. Once on the path he advanced cautiously, keeping close to the sides in case there were keepers still lurking. He passed the aviaries and heard the quiet crooning of cockatoos settling for the night. On the left was the little lake, empty now, the ducks and moorhens gathered under the willows or peacefully aground on the tiny rush-trimmed islands. Then he stopped.

Ahead of him lay a wide, rising sweep of grass, like an impassable sea between him and the shrubberies at the very top of the hill. Outlined against the sky he could see the bandstand, but the wide expanse of turf was broken only by an occasional tree. There was no cover for a hedgehog, let alone a boy. Henry hesitated. Behind him lay a quick dive through the shrubbery, then the lighted street and safety. Before him lay an uphill dash over the bare sweep of grass with for all he knew half-a-dozen keepers waiting to trap him, and the risk of capture.

Behind him came a high, shrill cry. Henry had started and was nearly halfway up the slope before he found himself thinking, "A bird—it must have been a bird!" By then it was too late to turn back. He was running blindly and when at last he reached the brow of the hill he had lost sight of the path and had to break wildly in among the dense shrubbery, where he stopped at last, gasping and straining for breath. He had to wait for his panting to subside before he could even listen. When he did, there was nothing to hear. He hardly even knew what he had *expected* to hear.

He groped among the bushes, feeling their cold, leathery touch on his hot skin, and then at last he was standing triumphant on the path—the very path! He looked in both directions, and almost immediately stopped feeling triumphant and was, for the first time, afraid. He really was alone in the park. A sudden gust of wind set the trees creaking high up among their bare bones, and a sheet of newspaper nearby unfurled, reared on end then sank slowly. At that moment Henry almost *wished* for a keeper. A hand clapped on his shoulder would have seemed almost friendly.

He set off up the path away from the lighted

street that he could still see on his left. A minute later he was at the seat where he had found Josh that morning, methodically folding his newspapers while the sun struck fire from his dewy beard.

Nervously Henry parted the bushes behind the seat. Seeing nothing, he pushed his way farther among the thick laurels, wildly, so that their branches sprang round him like live things. His knee struck something hard. He turned to his left and had found what he was looking for. Not one, but both of them, still piled high, crouching silently with humped backs like some strange, prehistoric beasts. Henry touched one—Josh's, he felt sure—and felt the cold of tarpaulin. He lifted it, and could make out the faint, whitish blur of the newspapers, and beneath it piles of boxes, neatly stacked. He dropped the cover. It did not really occur to him to find out what was *in* the boxes, to look for clues.

He had found them, and that was enough. Josh and Caleb, whatever mysterious night train had carried them off into the darkness, would be back. And Henry would find them—of that he was certain.

With a great upsurge of excitement he thrust back the laurels and was on the path, racing like a mad thing toward the iron rim of the railings, racing now not out of fear, but joy, absolute joy.

Chapter 3

$\mathcal{N}$ext morning Henry's first call was to the park. The barrows, as he had half expected, had gone. To Henry this mattered not at all.

"Where there's a barrow there's a Josh," he chanted to himself as he hurried down toward the town. "Where there's a barrow there's a Caleb!"

He had not the least idea where to begin looking for them, and yet now he felt certain of finding them. The clock struck ten as he went through the marketplace, the pigeons took to the air in a gray-blue whirl, and now they suddenly seemed like signs to Henry, too.

He went down to the canal again, for no real reason. It was only as he approached the triple-arched railway bridge that he knew the reason. He had found them.

He saw the barrows first, drawn up side by side under the middle arch, the one that stood with one foot on the green verge and the other in the water. Under the first arch, the one that spanned the road

and pavement, were Josh and Caleb themselves. They were bending over something with their backs turned, so Henry had the chance to take in the situation before they saw him.

An official-looking red and white sign saying

DANGER MEN AT WORK stood on the pavement a few
yards away from them. Henry saw that what Josh
and Caleb were so deeply engrossed in was a hole. It
was impossible for Henry to judge the depth of it
from where he stood, but it looked a good large one,
definitely of the kind that merited a red and white
DANGER notice.

19

"It's a water main, I tell you," he heard Caleb say. "It's enough to make your hair stand on end, Josh, the way you bring that pick down. We could've had water sprouting forty foot into the air. Missed it by half an inch, you did, half an inch! Just go *steady* with that pick."

"Half an inch is plenty," replied Josh comfortably. "Half an inch or half a mile—what's the difference as long as I missed it? Anyhow, I've done with the pick now."

He let it clatter to the pavement to prove it.

"Best thing is to get down there and finish off with shovels. Get the pipe clear. It looks good at the bottom of a hole, a pipe does. I always like to see a pipe—makes things look better for the public. There's a whole lot more *point* to a hole with a pipe than there is to one without, and it's my opinion we were lucky to strike it."

"Lucky to *miss* striking it," said Caleb. "If we *had* struck it——"

"I know," said Josh. "Water forty foot in the air. Now let up worrying, Caleb, and let's get this hole tidied up so's we can get down to the real business. You jump down and I'll hand you your shovel."

Caleb jumped down—he *flashed* down like a weasel into a burrow. For a moment he disappeared completely. Next minute his white face and foxy hair shot startlingly up over the edge of the hole and his eyes were looking right between Josh's sackcloth gaiters and straight into Henry's own.

Henry stood locked. Dumbly he stared back into

those pale, accusing eyes. Josh, evidently scenting danger, turned.

"Hello," he said, "it's that young feller. Remember, Caleb, that young feller we met in the park? Name of——?"

"Henry," said Henry, surprised to find that he had a voice and that it still worked. "Good morning."

"Good morning," agreed Josh.

Caleb said nothing. His hands now appeared one on each side of his face and Henry wondered nervously if he were preparing to spring.

"We was just digging a hole," explained Josh, waving a hand that indicated it and Caleb together.

"Yes," said Henry. "It looks a good one."

"Looks like a proper one, does it?" asked Josh anxiously. "I mean a *professional* hole? Caleb and me, we're not really——"

"Josh!" Caleb began to scramble up.

"Come and have a proper look down," invited Josh. "See what you think."

Henry approached. He peered over to see a hole about a yard square, with straight-cut edges and, just visible at the bottom, the reddish-brown gleam of a water main. Altogether, the hole was a great relief to Henry. He had no idea what he had expected to see down it, but it was certainly nothing as harmless and every day as this.

"Josh!" came Caleb's voice again. "Watch your step!"

"He's a member of the public, ain't he?" argued

Josh. "If he says it'll do, it'll do, and no more time wasted. Will it do?"

"Looks like any other hole in the road to me," said Henry, keeping his voice casual. "What's supposed to be special about it?"

He saw Josh and Caleb exchange triumphant glances.

"Nothing," said Caleb quickly. "Just some work we're doing on the water mains, eh, Josh?"

The answer was inaudible. Just then a train went over in a long, deafening thunder. Henry's hands went instinctively to his ears, but he saw that Josh and Caleb stood unperturbed—not so much as a flinch went over their faces. When the train had gone and the noise died away, it was as if a slate had just been wiped clean.

To Henry everything suddenly seemed amazingly simple. He looked straight at Josh and said, "Don't worry. I won't tell anyone about your hole."

There was a long silence. Josh and Caleb looked at each other. Then:

"I told you!" snapped Caleb fiercely. "I told you yesterday!"

"That was in the park, though," protested Josh. "All we was doing was ticking. There's no harm to a bit of a chat when you're out ticking."

"No harm?" Caleb's voice rose to near cracking point. "No *harm*? With the hole dug, hut ready for up—and the game up before we've so much as lit a fire?"

"He's not telling, though, that's the point, Caleb," said Josh patiently.

Caleb seemed not to hear. He was staring despondently down into the hole where his shovel still lay by the half-exposed water main.

"One of the best holes we've ever dug, I reckon," he said bitterly. "Would've fooled anyone. It'd got everything, that hole had—pipe and all. And all for nothing!"

"Now come on, Caleb," said Josh, "don't drop into the glooms, or we *are* finished. Let's try looking at the thing sensible."

Caleb's head shot up.

"Sensible!" he cried. "*You* to say that to *me*!"

Josh said nothing.

"If only you wasn't so soft, Josh," Caleb went on. Both of them seemed to have forgotten Henry's existence altogether. "I've told you a hundred times. Always picking up the odds and ends and talk, talk, talking to 'em. Like that policeman in Birmingham. Who would've believed it! A *policeman*!"

"But he was plainclothes," protested Josh. Caleb ignored him.

"And now *him*. Seen our hole before it's half dug and the whole game's finished."

Josh was silent again.

"I said I wouldn't tell," said Henry loudly, emboldened by Josh's shamefaced air to risk rousing the wrath of Caleb again. Caleb looked at him. He looked so worried and thoroughly downcast that

Henry came near to liking him.

"I dare say you won't," he said slowly at last.

"I *won't*," said Henry again. "I absolutely *won't*."

Caleb shook his head.

"Not the point really, is it, Josh?" he said.

"We-ell." Josh suddenly brightened. "It ain't, and then again it is, Caleb."

"What d'yer mean?" said Caleb.

"I mean *up till now* it ain't been the point," explained Josh, "but present circumstances permitting, it *might* be the point."

Henry, turning over this statement in his mind, could see that Caleb was at least as confused as he was.

"What I mean is," said Josh, lowering his voice, "that up till now we've took the night train the minute the public's got wind of us. But this here young feller's a bit of a different thing, to my mind."

"Why?"

"For one thing," said Josh, "he don't look like the public. For another, he don't *act* like the public. In a word, to my mind, he *ain't* the public."

Caleb stared at him.

"Not strictly speaking," added Josh, pressing his advantage. "The young 'uns is always on our side, Caleb, you know that."

"But this one knows about our hole," objected Caleb.

"I don't!" cried Henry then. He could contain himself no longer. "I don't know anything about your hole! I wish I did—oh, I just wish I did!"

They both stared at him.

"There you are," said Josh at last. "You heard what he said. He don't know *anything* when it boils down."

Caleb was looking wistfully again at the hole.

"It *is* a good hole," he said.

"Beautiful," agreed Josh.

"It'd be a downright crying shame to fill it in."

"Beyond all reason," said Josh.

Suddenly Caleb lifted his head and looked straight at Henry, just as the sun came out and set his hair alight.

"We're stopping!" he said defiantly. "We're stopping!"

Henry let out a long-held breath.

"Thank goodness!" he said. "Oh, thank goodness!"

Josh slapped his gaitered legs.

"Bravo, Caleb!" he cried. "Bravely spoke! Back down the hole and shovel away. We're stopping!"

Nimbly Caleb leaped back into the hole, then looked up at them, his face splintering into something very near a smile.

"Might as well give a hand, now he's here," he said. "Give him a bucket, Josh."

Next minute Henry, in a state of pure enchantment, was tipping the clayey soil as if he had been born to it. The three of them were conspirators now. Henry was on the same side of the fence.

Chapter 4

At the end of an hour the hole was finished to Caleb's satisfaction. The water main lay smooth and shining at the bottom and Josh ambled over to the barrows and came back with a red flag, which he hammered into the side of the hole.

"Just puts the finishing touch," he remarked. "We've never had anyone fall into any of our holes yet, have we, Caleb?"

Caleb was looking over Josh's shoulder.

"Public," he said briefly.

Henry knew his cue. He stuck his hands in his pockets and wandered off along the embankment. When he had gone a little way he stopped and searched for a few stones. He began to toss them idly into the water. As he did so two young women with baby carriages passed him, talking and laughing. Henry waited till they had gone a hundred yards or so, then turned and strolled back to the bridge. By then they were out of sight. The danger was past.

"Can't be too careful," remarked Josh as Henry rejoined them. "As long as you don't *draw* attention, you don't get it."

"Not many people come down here anyway," said Henry. "There's nothing to come for."

"That was what we reckoned," said Josh. "We always look over the bridges when we're ticking, and this was the best by a long stretch. The minute I set eyes on this bridge I could picture it with a hole under. Seemed made for it. I like a bit of green as well, and a bit of water."

"Now then," said Caleb briskly, "what about the hut?"

"Hut next," agreed Josh. "And a bite of dinner, p'raps?"

"I was thinking of an omelette. . . ." said Caleb.

"Perfect," said Josh. "One of them with the herbs . . . that French one you do."

"The Normandy," nodded Caleb. "But there's a snag."

"Snag?" queried Josh. He was collecting the tools and now carried them over to the barrows, where the others followed him.

"Eggs," explained Caleb. "No eggs. I shall have to 'ave a bit of a shop round, first. Do with some butter, too. And cheese."

"I can't put up this hut singlehanded," pointed out Josh.

"And pepper," went on Caleb. "We're clear out of that. And the anchovy essence is down to the last drop, and haddock's nowhere at all without anchovy, do what you will with it."

Josh was looking up over the roofs of the warehouses.

"It's a wet-looking sky up there," he observed. "And with this wind it'll be the kind of wet that gets right in under bridges. Once the rain gets a bit of a slant on it there'll be no keeping dry under this bridge. Hut first, shops later."

"All right," said Caleb, huffy now. "There's no *need* to have an omelette. There's no *need* for me to go fiddling for hours on end with dishes you'd be lucky to get even if you was king. There's no *need*. Beans on toast'll do me if it'll do you."

Josh looked miserably first at Caleb, then at the sky.

"I'll do the shopping," offered Henry.

They looked startled.

"If you just give me a list and the money it won't take long. I'll do it quicker than you would—I know the shops. Then you can get the hut up before it rains."

Caleb looked dubious but tempted. Josh was overjoyed.

"There!" he cried. "There's an offer for you! Hut and dinner both! Have your cake and eat it!"

He began to rummage in his barrow, took out a box and from it produced a makeshift pad of odd pieces of paper threaded together on a string. He took a pencil stub from his pocket, lifted a larger box from the barrow, sat on it and waited—evidently for Caleb to begin dictating.

"Butter, you said," he murmured, writing. "Eggs, pepper . . ."

"Anchovy sauce," said Caleb. "Mushrooms, a sprig o' parsley, a pound of tomatoes, and watch they don't give you the soft 'uns, a small——"

"Hold on, hold on!" cried Josh, scribbling furiously.

"A small chicken," continued Caleb relentlessly.

"Shall I get a frozen one?" asked Henry.

Now Caleb *did* stop. His white face drew itself into an expression that was by now becoming familiar to Henry. It was a sort of *shrunk* expression.

"Pardon?" he said, very distinctly.

"I said—shall I get a frozen one?" repeated Henry.

"In so far as I know," said Caleb, "there is no such thing as a frozen chicken. Chickens is either alive and laying eggs, or dead and on the table. That's nature, that is. But as to frozen——"

"My mother always gets frozen ones," said Henry.

He was dimly beginning to perceive that he must either stand up to Caleb in the early stages of their acquaintance or else be trodden on forevermore.

"She says they're just——"

He broke off. Josh, seated behind Caleb, was pulling the most extraordinary faces, which coupled with vigorous shakings of the head left no doubt at all of what he was trying to convey.

"Well, all right, then," said Henry. "An ordinary chicken."

Caleb nodded, mollified.

"He got strong views on cooking, you see," explained Josh apologetically. "That all, then, Caleb?"

"Do for now," said Caleb. "Did we *ought* to let him go, Josh? What if he don't come back?"

"He'll come back," said Josh. "Liked the look of him first time I saw him. More or less counted him as a sign."

Henry was by now used to being discussed as if he were not there. He could even understand Caleb's point of view.

"Don't worry," he said. "I'll come back. I'd like to see anyone stop me."

Josh beamed.

"There you are!" he said. "You've got no trust in human nature, Caleb, that's your drawback. Now here's the money, here's the list and here's a shopping bag. Watch the handles, one of 'em seems a bit shaky. Going to be useful you are, young feller. Nice there being three of us for a change."

Caleb said nothing. All the way along the embankment Henry could feel his pale suspicious eyes boring into his back. He did the shopping as quickly as he could, but it was nearly an hour before he turned on to the canal road again and with enormous relief saw that they were still there. Even now he could not feel quite sure of them.

As he drew nearer he could see that a kind of hoop-shaped canvas hut had been erected in his absence. It sat snugly under the middle arch on the narrow strip of green, and Henry could see Josh and Caleb nearby, busy with their unpacking.

Caleb pounced on the shopping bag the minute Henry set it down and swiftly checked off the items, examining each with care if not actual suspicion. He even opened the bag of tomatoes and felt them, one by one. Henry was glad he had remembered to ask for firm ones. He would not have liked to see Caleb confronted by a pound of squashy tomatoes.

"That's all right, then," said Caleb, satisfied at last. "Any change?"

Henry handed it over and Caleb counted it and

handed it to Josh saying, "Yours, Josh. I'll get the stove lit."

He disappeared into the hut. Henry, left alone with Josh, decided to ask some of the questions he had thought of during the past hour.

"What are you going to do with the hole now that you've dug it?" he began.

Josh looked up from his sorting. Henry noticed that the boxes seemed to contain paper, mostly.

"Oh, the hole's done with, now it's dug," he said. "It's just a bit of background, as you might say. It'll just stop there till it gets filled in again."

"And when will that be?" asked Henry.

"When we flits," explained Josh. "When we've finished."

"Will it be very long?" persisted Henry.

"Can't say. But I liked the way this town ticked, or we shouldn't have gone to the trouble to dig a hole in the first place. We should've stuck it out for a few nights in the park."

Henry considered this. Light began to dawn.

"You mean you've dug a *hole* so that you can put up the *hut*!" he cried. The whole amazing pattern was beginning to fall into shape.

Josh lowered his voice.

"You see, if we was to go putting up huts all over the place, there'd be questions asked. There'd be police and Authority on us before we'd so much as got the stove lit. But a hut with a *hole*, ah, that's a different matter!"

Henry, delighted, could see that it was.

"It blends in with the background natural, d'ye see," Josh went on. "Just dig a hole and put up a red flag and you could camp till doomsday and not a question asked. Worked it out a few years back, we did, the summer Caleb got pneumonia park-sleeping."

"It's marvelous!" cried Henry. "Absolutely marvelous!"

"It's beating 'em at their own game," said Josh, "that's the way we look at it. Dozens of holes we've dug, the long and broad of England, and not so much as the bat of an eyelid. You could dig one outside the Houses of Parliament, if you'd a mind to, and as long as nobody fell in it, there'd be no questions asked. That's what you got to watch. If anyone was to fall in, you'd have the Authorities on you and the game *would* be up."

Henry saw his opening.

"What game?" he asked. "What do you do?"

"Do?" said Josh. "I wouldn't rightly say that we do anything. It's more a matter of what we *are* than what we *do*."

"What are you, then?" pressed Henry desperately.

Josh hesitated. Then: "Night watchmen," he said at last. "That's what we are. Night watchmen."

Henry stared at him.

"Among other things," added Josh.

As Henry opened his mouth Caleb's thin face poked from the hut.

"*He*'s not stopping, is he?" he said. "There ain't enough herbs for three."

Henry, startled, looked at his watch.

"Lunch!" he cried. "I'm late! Back this afternoon!"

He had gone only a few yards when he heard Josh. He turned.

"Supper!" called Josh. "Come to supper! Seven sharp!"

Henry nodded. Somehow he would manage it.

"Seven!" he called back. "Thank you!"

All the way home he was so preoccupied with inventing a convincing reason for his lateness that he did not have time to wonder what Josh had meant by that last mysterious statement, just before Caleb had interrupted them. Which was just as well. Henry had had about as much mystery as he could stand for the time being.

Chapter 5

It was not very difficult after all to get away that evening. It was the night Henry usually went down to the church hall for a game of table tennis, and when he left the house just after half-past six there were no explanations at all to be made. His mother had taken it for granted that he was going there as usual, and did not seem to have noticed that he had eaten very little at teatime. Henry was glad of this, though he admitted to himself that if he had had to do some inventing, he would have done it without a qualm.

Already his acquaintance with Josh and Caleb was having a very strange effect on his perspectives. His home, for instance, simply did not seem like home any more. In the space of two days it had become merely a place where he unfortunately had to put in an appearance from time to time in between visits to the place where he felt he *really* belonged—with Josh and Caleb.

The idea of mentioning them to his parents was obviously unthinkable. He could see that they were broad-minded as parents go, in that they allowed him to watch unsuitable programs on television and go camping by himself in the summer, but there was not the least chance of their approving of the night watchmen. When he really thought about it, Henry was not yet certain that he *approved* of them himself. For the time being he was content simply to like them, with every hope that eventually he would come to approve of them as well.

After all, he told himself as he began to follow the now familiar route from home to canal, digging holes in pavements might be illegal, but it did nobody any harm—unless, as Josh pointed out, somebody fell in. Henry hoped fervently that nobody would fall in this particular one.

It was dark by the time Henry reached the embankment. The badly lit road had been made magical by rain. Shadows and puddles, black and silver, ran wetly together. Under each lamp lay a broad lake of brilliant light. And there, under the dark outline of the bridge, he could see the tiny red speck of the brazier and the faint outline of the hut. For a few seconds his mind reeled at the sheer impossibility of it all.

Then he was close enough to see the comfortable, shadowy interior of the hooped hut, with the warm glow of the fire lighting the faces of Josh and Caleb, and once again it was all real to him—more real than anything he had ever known.

Coming into the shelter of the tunnel from the wet

night as their invited guest, Henry felt suddenly and unaccountably shy.

There was a rich, savory smell of cooking, and he could see plates, knives and forks neatly set out on an upturned box, with a jar of catkins as a centerpiece. Josh, evidently in honor of the occasion, had removed his battered hat, though Henry had by now decided that he must sleep in it (it had certainly been drenched with dew that first morning in the park). He wore a dashing red and white spotted scarf tucked into his coat, his beard seemed almost tamed and altogether he had gone to some trouble to play the part of host. When he looked up and saw Henry standing hesitantly at the mouth of the arch, his face lit into welcome.

"Here we are!" he cried. "Here's the young feller, Caleb. Step inside and have a seat while we wait on the chicken."

He indicated a wooden box draped with what looked like another of Josh's neckerchiefs, only this one was green and white. Henry sat down. All three of them sat there looking out past the glow of the fire to the blackness beyond. It was a comfortable feeling. Josh and Caleb were evidently used to such silences, and Henry, listening to the soft stirring of coals in the brazier and the soughing of the wind under stone arches, was for the first time conscious of the charms of the life of a night watchman. He rested his arms on his legs as Josh and Caleb did and sat there taking it all in. After a while, with still no sign of the silence being broken, he turned his gaze to the interior of the hut itself. Already, after only a few hours, it looked like home.

The part where they were sitting was obviously the kitchen and living area, and Henry supposed that they slept somewhere at the back. He could not be quite certain without turning right round, so he contented himself with a close scrutiny of the part that he could see.

The sides of the tent (for that was what it really was, being made of canvas, over iron hoops) were lined with neat cupboards made from boxes with hinged lids and hooks to keep them closed. On one side a wooden strip had been fixed between two hoops and from it was suspended an array of saucepans and cooking pots of all shapes and sizes, all spotlessly scoured and very surprising in their sheer number. In Henry's own experience of camping, a frying pan, a saucepan and a kettle had been the sum total of utensils in use, with the emphasis very much on the frying pan.

Beneath the saucepans was fixed a shelf which did double duty as a storage space for crockery and a washstand, judging by the half-silvered mirror, bar of soap and enameled mug containing two toothbrushes and a tube of paste. Henry supposed that as Caleb was cook, this part of the hut was his domain, and he turned his attention to the side where he himself was sitting.

That, unmistakably, was Josh's. For one thing, it

was a good deal less tidy, being littered with paper of all kinds, loose pieces, pads, exercise books and even used envelopes. Screwing up his eyes in the dim light, Henry could make out that some of it was covered with large, scrawly handwriting and some of it was typewritten. On the wall were pinned a calendar, a picture of a harbor and what looked like a railway timetable. Hung from hoop to hoop was a small bookshelf, and Henry could make out the titles of *The Bible* and *The National Dictionary* on the largest of the volumes. He would have to wait for daylight to investigate the others.

A faint vibration began to stir in the stones above them. They all cocked their heads, listening. As the tremor changed to a distant roar and the roar to a deafening thunder, Henry's hands went up to his ears, and even in the midst of the dizzying swirl of sound he noticed again that Josh and Caleb sat quite still, unperturbed as if it were the mere buzzing of a bluebottle.

"That'll be the six thirty-five from Lincoln," remarked Josh when the echoes had sunk back into the stones. "Dishing up time, Caleb."

Caleb rose, and for the first time Henry noticed the stove that was just outside the hut, near the bridge wall. He had more or less taken it for granted that the brazier was used for cooking, but it was becoming apparent that Caleb went in for a good many unexpected refinements. The stove was a neat, modern-looking affair with two burners on top and what looked like a small oven underneath. Josh saw him looking at it.

"It's gas," he said. "You could cook *anything* on it. Won't blow up, either, Caleb says. Will it, Caleb?"

"Will it what?" Caleb was peering into saucepans again, delicately wielding the salt.

"Blow up," said Josh. There was an anxious note in his voice that told Henry that the question was more than merely rhetorical.

"If I've told you once I've told you a thousand times."

Caleb was ranging up three plates now, and beginning to serve. His nose twitched enthusiastically, he was all fox again.

"There," said Josh, "I told you. Never blow up in a thousand years, that won't. We like to keep it just outside, though—just in case, you know. Not that it'd ever happen."

Henry began to wonder how Josh ever summoned up any appetite at all for his meals, living as he obviously did in constant terror of being blown sky high before he so much as got a knife and fork into them. Just then one of the gas jets flared noisily and they both jumped. Caleb turned it off.

"Got to keep up with the times," said Josh, but his voice was wistful.

The meal that followed was a feast—and not only because it was being eaten in a night watchman's hut under a railway bridge. There was chicken, delicately simmered with mushrooms in rich, herb-flavored juices that were so disturbingly delicious that in the end Henry copied the others and mopped them up eagerly with his bread—despite a lifetime's warnings that this was never to be done in public. For dessert there was lemon meringue pie—Henry's own favorite—lighter and tangier than he had ever known it, and as the last delicious morsels of his second helping melted upon his tongue, he cried, "That was marvelous! It was the best meal I've ever had in my whole life!"

Caleb's sharp face bloomed in the warm light of the brazier into a surprising softness, mingled with something else that was almost shyness.

"Liked it, did you?" he said, clearing his throat.

"Liked it!" echoed Henry. He had always been impressed by good food—it meant a good deal to him.

Caleb, to hide his confusion, got up and began clearing the dishes. Josh jerked his head confidentially toward the other's back.

"Takes his cooking to heart, Caleb does," he said. "He really threw himself into that stew."

In a louder voice he said, "You leave that washing up, Caleb, and sit down while I make the tea. Then we can all have a nice talk."

Henry's heart jumped a beat. The cat, at last, was to be let out of the bag.

Chapter 6

"We could light the lamp," said Josh as they sat with their fingers curved round their steaming mugs of tea. The wind was getting up in earnest now, and the warmth from the brazier was being blown the wrong way. "We could, but there's no sense in it."

"Waste not, want not," said Caleb. "You don't need light for talking. And the police'll be down here before the night's out. Bound to be."

"Why?" asked Henry, alarmed.

"Police is down *all* roads, some time in the night," Josh told him. "Bound to be. Their job. But we're all square and tidy here. Four red lamps round the hole and two danger notices. If all holes was as well looked after as ours, the police'd be in clover. Bright pink clover."

"But yours isn't a real hole," said Henry. "I mean—" he hesitated, "I mean, it's an illegal one."

Caleb's head shot up.

"It never is!" he cried. "What next! Illegal!"

"There ain't an actual law about it," explained

Josh. "Leastways, not that we know of. Not in as many words. If they'd come to think of it, they'd have *made* a law. But they ain't come to think of it—yet. Caleb says there'll have to be a Bill in the Houses of Parliament if anyone falls in one of our holes. That's why we have to be so particular, see."

Henry did see. In his own mind he felt sure that there must be *some* law that discouraged people from going about digging up pavements whenever they felt like it, but he did not pursue the point. Josh and Caleb obviously did not like to think of themselves as lawbreakers.

"We should get moved *on* if the police was to get wind of us," said Caleb, "that I don't deny. And moved on's just what we don't want to be."

"We ain't even started yet," put in Josh. "To-morrow we start."

"Er—start?" prompted Henry, hardly daring.

The other two looked at each other.

"Go on, Josh, tell him," said Caleb. "No harm now. That boy knows enough already to send us running for the night train without so much as time to lace our boots. No harm in knowing the rest. Harm's already done."

"It's getting hold of the place," explained Josh then. "That's what I'm after."

"Getting *hold* of it?" said Henry.

"In black and white," said Josh. "Which is the nearest you can ever get hold of anything, really. It's for this book I'm writing."

He waved his hand in Henry's direction and the meaning of the confused heaps of paper suddenly became clear. Clear yet incredible. Henry stared at Josh, with his thick boots, mittened fingers, rope belt and Elijah's beard, and tried to take in the undreamed-of fact that he was an actual author, a writer of books.

"Been writing it for years, he has," put in Caleb, not without pride. "Not that it'll ever get finished."

"Oh no," agreed Josh comfortably. "It'll never get finished. Can't."

"Why can't it?" asked Henry.

"Too much to go into it," explained Josh. "It's about *places*, you see. And places is one thing you can never run out of—the world being the size it is."

"Thousands of pages he's wrote," put in Caleb again, more talkative on the subject of Josh's authorship than Henry would have believed possible. "Thousands and thousands. Typed, too, most of it. He's got a typewriter I give him for his birthday a couple of years back. Show him, Josh."

Josh pointed toward one of the cupboards on his side of the tent, and Henry saw a small, shabby case half concealed by Josh's discarded hat.

"I shouldn't be surprised," went on Caleb, "if he hasn't wrote as many pages as William Shakespeare. And all about places. Here, there and *everywhere* he's wrote about."

"And this place next!" cried Josh eagerly. "Full of words, this place is. I can feel 'em coming out of the top of my head!"

Looking at him now, eyes alight and beard gone wild again, Henry was quite prepared to see that very thing happen.

"It's a sort of guide book, is it?" he asked.

"Guide book?" said Caleb.

"Well, you said it was about places," said Henry. "I mean, well, what's it for?"

For a moment neither answered. They looked genuinely nonplused.

"I don't rightly think you could say it was *for* anything," replied Josh slowly at last. "It just *is*."

Henry, in his turn, was left with nothing to say. In the end, though, feeling that another silence was about to set in unless he acted quickly, he said, "What you mean is, you're writing it for the *sake* of writing it."

"Yes!" cried Josh. "That's just it. That's absolutely it." He stared fondly at the muddled heaps of paper. "Do as you please," he murmured.

The phrase struck a chord.

"That's what you said the other day," said Henry, "in the park."

"That's right," agreed Josh. "Do-as-you-pleasers, that's what we are. And now you know."

Henry by no means knew all that he wanted to know.

"And where are you from?" he asked. Again there was the swift exchange of glances.

"There," replied Josh guardedly.

"There?" repeated Henry.

"You've got Here," explained Josh, waving an

arm, "and you've got There. We're from There."

"And where's There?" asked Henry. The question sounded foolish, even to him.

"Ah," said Josh, "that you'd have to take the night train to find out. And take the night train is something you'll never do, young feller. Because you belong Here."

Henry pondered.

"But anyone can take a night train," he said.

"Not this one, they can't," said Caleb with satisfaction. "She's private, this one is. *She*'s not on any timetables, oh no! She comes whistling out of the dark when folks is in their beds and the most they'll see of her is her green eyes and the red fires blowing up her smoke."

"Fires!" cried Henry. "A *steam* engine!"

"She comes to our whistle the long and broad of England," Josh said. "She can weave her way through the junctions like a homing pigeon. Under the tunnels and over the moors, up dale and down river. Keeps the rails polished on the branch lines and can skirt a town with never a signal-box man to know. She's a rare, secret one she is, though you'd never guess it from the noise of her—clap and gallop and thunder with whistles fit to raise up the dead— oh, she's a beauty, she is!"

Henry sat picturing the wayward train on its private journeys, untamed by timetable, unknown to junction box and signal-watching stationmaster. The railroads of England became suddenly for him uncharted country, a wilderness past all dreams of the neat, methodical diesels that he knew.

"Only nights she travels," Josh went on. "Come daylight, and she'll draw by in a quiet cutting—hundreds there are, if you know where to look for 'em. Somewhere with high banks full of nettles, away from all bridges—that's where she likes to browse."

"Except when she goes back There," said Caleb. "Has to go back There sometimes, for a fettling. Get her brasses rubbed up bright and her wheels oiled."

"Vain as a peacock that one is," broke in Josh, "for all she never travels but by night. But in a full moon—ah, *then* you can see how she shines. Caleb and me we stand up there and can see them shining rails come feeding up out of the dark and her breath goes up like the smoke was turned to silver and the wind over the top comes rushing into your mouth like jugfuls of cold water and—grand, it is. Beautiful."

They sat there for a time, Caleb and Josh deep in memories of their night rides, Henry aching with the longing that he himself might one day—or night —go with them, taste the freedom of a wild train carelessly ranging the railroads of England by its own secret byways.

"And that's how you get from Here to There?" he asked at last.

"It's the only way," replied Josh. "If it wasn't for that night train, Caleb and me would be landed Here forevermore. That's why we camp under bridges, see. That's why we get the night timetables off by heart every blessed place we go. And once night falls, you won't find Caleb and me farther'n a whistle away from a railway line. It's the way out, see."

"But what if one night it didn't come?" asked Henry. "What if something went wrong?"

"*That ain't never got to happen*," said Caleb with awful emphasis.

As if for reassurance the now familiar stirrings began to run about the arch. Henry, with a tremendous effort, managed to keep his hands away from his ears. The noise half stunned him, but he managed it.

"The seven fifty-three from Grantham," remarked Josh. "Running three minutes late, I should say. Time to get tidied up for the night, Caleb."

Henry recognized his cue.

"I'd better go now," he said. "My mother will be wondering where I've got to."

"We don't want that," said Caleb. "Boys is bad enough, but their mothers is worse."

"He's got a nasty bark," Josh explained to Henry, "but his bite's not worth mentioning. You'll find out."

"Thank you for the supper," said Henry. He brightened at the very memory of it. "It was the best meal I've ever had in my whole life. And good luck tomorrow. Will you be starting early?"

"Dawn," said Josh briefly. "At the absolute crack."

Henry hung back for a moment, half hoping for an invitation to act as guide. It did not come.

"Good night, then," he said.

"Good night." They spoke in unison, lifting their heads from the tasks they had already begun. Henry, standing on the other side of the brazier, already felt himself cut off from them. He took a last look at them in the reddish-lit interior of their hut, and then turned his face to the windy wet and silver of the canal road toward home.

Chapter 7

H enry was back at the canal bridge by ten o'clock the next morning. He hardly really expected to find either of them there, but as he approached, Caleb emerged from the hut with a saucepan in his hand and, seeing Henry, waved the other arm in salute.

"Morning," he said. He was wearing a large butcher's apron with various spoons and skewers stuck in the belt like weapons.

"Good morning," said Henry. "Did you sleep all right?"

"Half," replied Caleb. "Half and half."

"The trains must be a bit disturbing," said Henry. "Though I expect you're used to that."

"The trains is nothing," said Caleb. "But when we're on night watch we sleep one at a time, see. I sleep half the night and Josh sleeps the other. When you got a hole you got to keep an eye on it."

"I suppose you have," agreed Henry. Caleb went back into the hut and took down a pair of scales. Then rows of bags and packets were set out on the makeshift table. "Is Josh in town?"

Caleb nodded.

"Ticking," he said. "And getting his letters posted. Half the night writing letters, as usual."

"Can you send letters from Here to There?" asked Henry, surprised. He had not thought of There as being a *postal* address.

"He ain't sending letters There," said Caleb, "he's sending 'em Here. Droves of 'em. Letters of introduction, he calls 'em. Letters to the Mayor, letters to the churches, letters to the schools—all typed, mind you, on proper notepaper. *Joshua M. Smith*, he signs himself, and he's no more a Smith than I am. He overdoes things, that's his trouble. Never knows when to stop. One of these days he *will* go too far."

Caleb was measuring ingredients and talking at the same time. Cooking evidently loosened his tongue.

"What are the letters for?" asked Henry.

"Telling 'em he's coming to see 'em," said Caleb.

"*See* them?" cried Henry. "See the Lord Mayor?"

"Oh, he always has a word with the Lord Mayor," said Caleb, turning his ingredients into a bowl and adding water out of a large, stoppered container. Henry, trying to picture Josh in his sackcloth gaiters and incredible hat, climbing the white stone steps to the town hall, felt his own legs positively tremble.

"But what does he *tell* them?" he gasped.

"The truth, o' course." Caleb was unconcernedly peeling mushrooms. "Not much taste in these, there'll be. Black, mushrooms should be, not these prettified town things."

"The *truth*!" Henry actually did have to sit down now.

"He tells 'em he's an author visiting the town for a book he's writing," said Caleb. "That's the truth, ain't it?"

Henry was bound to agree that it was. Only partly, of course, but as far as it went—the truth.

"I'll just drop the flaps a minute," said Caleb conversationally. "Stay tight."

He moved forward and loosened the tapes that held back the canvas flaps at the front of the hut.

"Back soon," he said, and was gone. Henry sat mystified. He could hear metallic-sounding clangs nearby as if tools were being moved. Soon he could hear, too, slow footsteps approaching, passing for a moment, then going away. They were drowned then by the sound of a train going overhead. Henry, despite the fact that the night watchmen were not there to notice, kept his hands from his ears. This time it did not seem so bad. He let the din wash over him. When it had gone, he was left with first a faint roaring in his ears, then complete silence. The flaps lifted and Caleb came back in.

"Safety first," he said, and resumed the peeling of his mushrooms.

"Who was it?" asked Henry.

"Public," said Caleb. "Spotted him too late for you to peg off. Don't do for boys to be seen in night watchmen's huts. There's too many busybodies about asking questions. Not to mention the——" he broke off suddenly. The knife stopped paring mushrooms. Then, "Just went out and sorted a few tools," he went on as if he had not broken off at all. "Makes things seem a bit realistic if you move tools about now and then."

Henry nodded. He looked round the hut again, noticing things that he had missed the night before. There was the bed at the far end, the one where Josh and Caleb took turns, half and half. Remembering the books, he turned to study the titles. *Medical Who's Who*, he read. *Whitaker's Almanack. Places of Interest to Visit in the East Midlands*. Even telephone directories.

"How does Josh know *where* to write?" he asked, suddenly thinking he might have put two and two together.

"Them, for one thing," said Caleb, jerking his head toward the books. "Then there's the newspapers. Find out who the big nobs are. You can get the parsons off church bulletin boards. There's plenty of ways and means. When we're out ticking, he nips into telephone kiosks, see. Looks up names and addresses and writes 'em down. Just one or two at a time. Can't hang round too long in kiosks without folks rapping on the glass and questions getting asked."

"You've certainly worked it all out," said Henry admiringly.

"You learn as you go along," replied Caleb. "There's always new ideas cropping up."

"If your name isn't Smith," said Henry, "what is it?"

"Surname, you mean?" asked Caleb. Henry nodded.

"Got none," said Caleb. "Nobody There's got one. Don't believe in 'em. And have one Here!" He shuddered, put down the knife and began rummaging in his store cupboards. "The minute you got a surname, you're ticketed, that's the way we look at it. They'd have your name filled in on forms and wrote on lists before you could say jackknife. Josh and Caleb, that's us. *That* won't be filled in on no forms."

"But Josh calls himself Smith," said Henry. "People could easily check up on him."

Caleb turned and fixed him with suddenly wicked and triumphant eyes.

"Easy?" he said. "You ever gone through the Smiths in a telephone book? *Blinding*, that's what it is. Smith, Smith, Smith, page after page and your eyes turning somersaults before you're down the first column of 'em. J. Smith, that's Josh—the safest name in England."

Henry sat silent, marveling at the simplicity and ingenuity of it all.

"Hsssh!" hissed Caleb sharply—and unnecessarily.

Henry heard nothing. Caleb darted out from the hut again, dropping the flaps behind him. A few moments later Henry heard the footsteps, then again the clanking of tools on the pavement. When Caleb reappeared he was frowning.

"Same feller," he said. "Didn't catch his face, but I didn't like the look of him."

"Why not?" asked Henry. "What was wrong with him?"

"I didn't like the look of him," repeated Caleb obstinately. "You can't have ticked places the number of years I have without knowing if you like things or not, straight off."

"What *is* ticking?" asked Henry, more to change the subject than anything else, because he thought he knew the answer by now. "Is it sort of looking things over?"

Caleb paused for a moment before replying.

"It's seeing," he said, "and *feeling*. Both at the same time. It's—sniffing at a place, getting the scent of it. *Sensing* things."

Henry, watching the pale weasel face with its sharp eyes and thin, twitching nose, knew exactly what he meant. He could see, too, that Caleb really was worried.

"What's keeping Josh?" he muttered, getting up again and peering between the flaps. "Four hours he's been gone. Under a bus or worse he could be, gone all that time. What's that, just come round—*there* he is!"

He let the flaps drop.

"It'll be the death of me, this life," he said.

"But you're a do-as-you-pleaser, aren't you?" said Henry. "Why do you do it if it doesn't please you?"

Caleb whirled on him then, flashing with his old fire.

"It *does* please me!" he snapped.

"Oh!" said Henry. "I'm sorry."

Caleb snatched his packets and tins from the table and began to stow them noisily back into the cupboards.

"*Some*body's got to watch him," he said. "And if his own brother can't, who will?"

Henry did not answer. Conversation with Caleb in this mood was not easy.

"Dreaming along, watching pigeons and counting cracks in pavements," he went on. "Signs here and signs there, dreaming along with his head in the clouds. *Some*body's got to watch him."

Josh's face, red with pleasure, appeared between the flaps.

"Morning, young feller," he cried. "Good morning! Beautiful ticking this place's got. And full of clocks and bells, Caleb. Bells at every quarter, there is. I love bells. They're a sign, I always think."

Caleb looked at Henry. He didn't actually say "What did I tell you?" but it was written all over his quicksilver face.

"Come on, then," he said resignedly. "Sit down and I'll get some tea. Letters gone off?"

"Each and every," nodded Josh genially. "I could do with some tea, licking all them flaps and stamps. You going to do the shopping again, young feller?"

"Yes, of course," said Henry, "if you want me to."

Caleb paused by the door, kettle poised.

"*If* it's safe," he said. "That young feller down

here day and night could be the undoing of us, Josh."

"Nobody sees him," Josh protested. "Never *known* a road empty like this one. Perfect."

"You didn't happen to pass a feller as you turned off here, did you?" asked Caleb.

"Feller? Yes, I did," said Josh, puzzled.

"Twice he's been past here this morning," said Caleb.

Josh stared.

"There's nothing in that," he said. "He didn't see you, young feller, did he?"

"I shut the flap," Caleb told him. "But that ain't the point. I didn't like the looks of him, Josh."

A faint look of alarm appeared on Josh's face.

"You didn't?" he asked at last, uncertainly.

"No, Josh, I didn't," said Caleb with finality. "I only see his back, mind you, and backs can be deceiving. But mark my words. If that feller comes past here again, if it's the last thing I do, I'll get a look at the color of his eyes!"

"His eyes!" Josh cried. "But they lost track of us three towns back, at Basingfield! They can't be on our track already, Caleb! We've doubled twice since then to throw 'em off!"

Henry, watching them intently, was aware of being on the brink of discovering yet another mystery. Then, disconcertingly, he caught the full glare of Caleb's eyes.

"He's listening!" he snapped. "Drop it!" and was gone.

Chapter 8

$\mathcal{H}$enry was finding it difficult to take an interest in anything other than the night watchmen. Hours spent away from them were, to him, hours wasted. His mother, feeling sorry for him and thinking he might be bored, kept arranging all kinds of well-meant treats and outings that left Henry exhausted with frustration. That afternoon, for instance, he was taken to see a film, and the following day a whole day's outing was planned to visit a zoo fifty or sixty miles away. Henry, prowling ferociously past the cages, glared back at the captive beasts and knew exactly how they felt.

Today Josh had planned the first of his visits. Henry's mind became dizzy trying to speculate where he might have gone, whether he had been found out. There was even the possibility that when Henry arrived at the embankment the following day, the hole would be filled in, the hut gone, and Josh and Caleb vanished forever on the night train.

What actually *had* happened he found out sooner than he had expected. They had arrived home and were having a late tea, and his mother was reading the evening paper.

"Henry!" she cried. "Just listen to this. What a pity you weren't at school!"

"What?" asked Henry without enthusiasm.

" 'Author visits local school,' " she read out. " 'Pupils at Highgate School today had the opportunity of meeting an author in person. Mr. Joshua Smith, who is writing a book which will include a chapter about Mandover, was shown round the school by the headmaster, Mr. W. Reynolds. Afterward Mr. Smith talked to some of the older pupils and answered their questions. He told them that anyone who had ambitions to be an author should "Travel light, travel everywhere, and learn to watch for signs." He then autographed the children's books, writing in each, "A rose by any other name might not be a rose at all—Joshua M. Smith." Afterward the headmaster commented, "We were lucky to receive this unexpected visit from this interesting writer. The children will have learned much from it." Mr. Smith was vague about his future plans for gathering information about Mandover, but mentioned that he intended to go on various trips.' "

"He didn't say 'trips,' " Henry said. "He said 'ticks.' "

"Pardon, dear?"

"Nothing," said Henry.

"Isn't it wonderful, though? Fancy that! And what a shame you couldn't have been there. You'd have enjoyed that, dear."

Henry doubted it. Even now the vision of Josh being conducted round his school by the headmaster in person was enough to make him close his eyes in anguish.

"There's a picture as well," said his mother. "He does look quite an interesting person. And I suppose a beard's all right on an *author*. Mr. Reynolds has come out well, you can tell it's him at a glance. And isn't that John Payne in the background with his autograph book?"

Henry took the paper with a show of carelessness. It was Josh, all right. With a great rush of relief he saw that the hat, the rope belt and sackcloth gaiters were missing. At first glance Josh looked as ordinary and anonymous as you would expect someone to be who was being shown round a school by a headmaster. It was the sort of picture that Henry himself would not ordinarily give even a second glance. All the same, he did not like it. It meant that Josh was no longer under cover. He was out in the open now, and could be spotted—by over five hundred children from Henry's school, to begin with.

"I think I'll go down to the church hall for a bit tonight," he said, hoping that his voice did not tremble.

"Are you sure, dear? It's been a tiring day for you, that long journey and then trailing round the zoo. I should leave it till tomorrow."

Henry, cornered, had an inspiration.

"I want to hear about what happened at school

today," he said—with perfect truth, as it happened. "I want to hear what that author said."

"Well—I must say it does sound interesting. All right, dear, just for an hour, then. Would you like your father to pick you up in the car?"

"No!" Henry almost shouted. "No, thanks, Mother."

He fled. He took a bus down to the town center and ran all the rest of the way. An hour could be stretched to an hour and a half, but even that left little time.

At least they were still there. He saw the red speck of the brazier as soon as he rounded the corner into the canal road.

Josh and Caleb were having supper, and he saw them look up as they heard his approaching footsteps. They obviously could not see who it was until he arrived panting at the mouth of the arch, and he saw the relief on their faces.

"It's the young feller," said Josh. "You're in a hurry.

Henry, panting, held out the copy of the evening paper he had bought in the square on the way down.

"I—saw—this!" he gasped.

Caleb gave him a swift look and snatched the paper from him.

"What?" he snapped, peering in the dim light, his nose almost touching the paper.

"Page three. At the bottom."

Caleb opened it and a loose page fell unheeded in

his gravy. There was a very long silence. Caleb's face was hidden behind the newspaper. Josh picked up his knife and fork and got on with his supper. Henry noticed that he was wearing his old clothes again— even to the hat. The sight of him was comforting.

"He doesn't *look* much like the photograph," Henry thought. "Not really—except for the beard."

Caleb put the paper down. Seeing his face, Henry instinctively backed a couple of paces and found himself nearly on the brazier. Caleb's voice, when at last he did speak, was *clenched*.

"There he sits," he said, "mopping up his gravy without a care in the world. And here's his photograph splashed all over the papers for all England to read!"

"Oh, not all England!" cried Henry. "Only Mandover and Staithe."

Josh, interested, put down his knife and fork and took the paper. He was lost behind it for some time. When he finally did put it down his face, even considering the glow from the brazier, was red.

"That *is* a nuisance," he admitted.

"Nuisance!" Caleb's voice was rising now. "First day out, and you do this! After all I said to you last night. If they're after us, they've got us now, plump and square!"

"It don't *look* much like me, Caleb." Josh's voice was pleading. "They might not know it was me."

Caleb let out a snort of disgust and pushed his plate right away.

"I can't eat another bite," he said. "I've got stomach for nothing now. Might not know it was you! It's got your *name* wrote on it, hasn't it?"

"There's plenty of people called Smith," mumbled Josh. But he pushed his plate aside too.

"And *Joshua*, as well, I suppose?" said Caleb. "We might as well pack up and whistle for the night train straight off. If we get clear now, we might stand a chance of throwing them off again."

"You keep going on about *them*," argued Josh, "but how do you know they're on to us? Take things a bit easier, Caleb. A feller walks past here two times and you catch a sight of his back and don't like the looks of him. That don't make four to me. Two and two makes four, but that don't. Not to my mind."

Caleb was staring moodily into the fire and seemed hardly to hear him.

"Did you see him again today?" Josh asked.

Caleb shook his head.

"There you are, then," Josh said. "Just an ordinary feller taking an ordinary walk. *That's* four."

"All right," said Caleb, "suppose it wasn't one of them. Suppose it wasn't. What about all them children at the school. They'll know you again if they see you, if *I* know children."

"What of it?" asked Josh.

"Supposing one of 'em was to come down here and see you?" said Caleb. "What then? Authors don't live in huts watching holes, even children know that."

"Mmmmm." Josh pondered. Then his face lit up. "If one of 'em does come," he cried, "I say I'm down here talking to you. Asking questions, don't you see, for the book! That fits!"

Caleb looked dubious but slightly happier.

"We shall still have to be careful," he said.

"Oh, we will," agreed Josh. "I shall be very careful now, make no mistake. *Exceeding* careful. But don't let's pack up now, Caleb. I'm all set fair here. I was going to write it all up tonight." He looked wistfully toward his typewriter. "I've got some beautiful stuff."

Caleb shrugged, but Henry saw the softening of his face and knew that the victory was with Josh.

"Do as you please!" he said.

"That's right," cried Josh. "Do as you please! That's what we're here for! I could eat some dessert now, I think, Caleb. Apple dumpling?"

Caleb nodded.

"With custard?"

"I'll get it." Caleb stood up.

Henry sat and ate apple dumpling with them. The brazier sang and the wind was a mere hint of music in the arches. The newspaper lay forgotten in the darkness of the hut behind them. A long, beautiful silence set in.

Chapter 9

$\mathcal{N}$ext day Henry knew where Josh had gone, but knowing did not make him feel very much easier. Things had seemed safe and certain enough last night in the snugness of the hut, but broad daylight and streets full of people brought again the terrifying feeling of being in the open, no longer under cover. It was only at night when he knew that Josh and Caleb were in their hut under the arches and within whistle of the railway, that Henry really felt happy. After all, the hole had become part of the scenery now. If questions were going to be asked about it, they would have been asked by now.

He was worried, too, by the mysterious references to "them." Whoever "they" were, they were dangerous, old enemies who had hounded Josh and Caleb from place to place and even now might be mingling with the crowds in Mandover itself, ready to strike. Henry found himself looking at every face he passed, hoping that he might perhaps recognize one of "them" if he saw him, by the eyes. There was obviously something very odd about their eyes.

Henry had given a good deal of thought to what actually *could* be unusual about them, and had come to the conclusion that they must either be very small, very big, be three in number, or have a patch over one. By the time he had wandered through Mandover for an hour or so he had not seen a single one- or three-eyed person, but the eyes of practically everyone he met seemed either unusually small or unusually big.

His own eyes beginning to ache and spin, he resisted the temptation to go down to the canal bridge and see if Caleb was there, and went home. He realized that it was as well to put in an appearance there now and then.

He had intended to stay there until evening, but by the middle of the afternoon felt so restive and uneasy that despite himself he went down into Mandover again. He stood in the marketplace and stared desperately at the stone walls of the town hall as though if he stared hard enough and long enough his eyes would by some miracle make stone transparent. Somewhere in there was Josh, meeting the Lord Mayor. At this very moment he might be dropping some fatal hint, some chance remark, that would lead to discovery—perhaps, even, to arrest. There was a policeman on duty outside the town hall, as usual, and to Henry, watching him, his every movement seemed sinister and full of meaning. Once he went to the small blue police box nearby and was in there for several minutes, making a telephone call.

"He's calling up reserves," thought Henry, and it was all he could do to prevent himself from rushing up the steps to the now unguarded door and shouting a warning to Josh before it was too late. Just then the clock began to strike three, the pigeons went flapping out into the air and Henry, lifting his head to watch, saw Josh.

There was a narrow balcony running round the base of the clock dome, high up above the roof of the hall itself. No one ever used it—the big balcony, the one used for public occasions, was much lower down, and would hold thirty or forty people. But there was Josh lording it over the town, dwarfed though he was by the great clock face above him, and hardly bigger than the minute finger.

He was waving his arms about, excited, Henry guessed, by the bells and pigeons. The Lord Mayor stood beside him looking suitably *un*excited, even from this distance. Henry looked swiftly about him. Nobody else seemed to have noticed the pair. There was not a black patch in sight. Even so, he was relieved when Josh's lively figure disappeared through a small door in the wall and the pigeons went fluttering back to their ledges and everything was back to normal again.

Just before half-past three Josh emerged. Henry, throwing precautions to the wind, ran to meet him.

"Are you all right?" he gasped. "Is everything all right?"

"Steady, now, young feller," said Josh. "Take things easy. What's the rush?"

"I saw you up there by the clock," said Henry. "You must have been in there for hours."

"One of my best visits, that was," said Josh with satisfaction. "Pages of notes I got." He tapped his coat pocket. "And as for them bells and pigeons—*you* never known anything like it. The bells was swinging and thumping round us and pigeons clapping about thick as snowflakes—I never known the like, and that's a fact."

"Are you going back to the hut now?" asked Henry anxiously. He was keeping pace with Josh, striding easily now along one of the narrow streets that led in the direction of the canal. Josh stopped suddenly.

"Best turn back now, young feller," he said abruptly.

"Why?" asked Henry, startled.

Josh looked quickly about him and lowered his voice.

"Caleb thinks he's seen *him* again," he said. "Only got a look at the back of him, again, mind, but he's got a nose for that sort of thing, Caleb has. Safety first. Best for you not to be seen with me."

Henry nodded.

"I'll come down later," he said. "When it's getting dark."

"Take a good look about you before you come down there," warned Josh. "Come by a different way—act foxy and throw 'em off. If there's anyone following—don't come."

Henry shook his head. Josh's face was serious. There was danger then—real danger.

"I'll be careful," he promised.

He stood there and watched Josh set off alone, broad-backed, duck-footed, unable to look anonymous even in the shabby but plain clothes he used for visiting. Even from the back.

Henry pretended to look in the window of a

nearby shop and next time he looked up Josh had disappeared. It was almost a relief. Henry turned abruptly from the window and banged hard into a man who had been standing just behind him.

"I'm sorry," he began, looking up.

The man did not reply. He gave Henry a strange, blurred look and walked off in the same direction as Josh had taken. Henry stood staring after him, powerless to move. It was the eyes. These must have been the eyes Josh and Caleb had talked about—green, a pure, light, brilliant green such as Henry had never seen before in a human face—*cat's*-eye green, greener, even.

Red for danger . . . green for danger . . . confused warning messages ran through Henry's brain. By the time he had collected himself, the man had gone. It was too late now to warn the night watchmen. The route Josh had taken was by far the quickest to the canal bridge. However hard Henry ran, there was no chance of his getting there first. He looked nervously about him, half expecting to find himself met by a battery of glaring, light-green eyes. People hurried past, their faces blank, wrapped-up and everyday—blue-eyed, brown-eyed, *safe*-eyed faces. Henry gave a quick shiver, turned and headed for home. For once, he was glad to.

He did not set off for the canal that evening until it was dusk. He wore his dark mackintosh, meaning to keep close into the shadows, merging himself with the darkness as nocturnal creatures do, using the night as a cover. He did not pass through the market-place at all. He wove an intricate pattern through the familiar network of narrow streets, stopping by every corner for the sound of a following footfall, doubling now and again into alleyways, playing mouse to an invisible cat.

When he finally reached the canal embankment he was right on the far side of the bridge, approaching it from the opposite direction. There was no bright speck of brazier tonight, only a faint red glow illumining the center arch to tell him that they were still there, and as he drew nearer, the reflectors of the lamps round the hole.

He advanced cautiously, throwing frequent glances back over his shoulder, running past the lamps to reach the safety of the pools of darkness between. He wore rubber-soled shoes and made no more sound than if he were walking on moss or turf.

At last he reached the bridge and crept through the center arch to the front of the hut. The flaps were closed and light spilled from the cracks to mingle with the ruddy glow of the brazier. Henry listened and heard, almost immediately, the comforting chink of cutlery—knives and forks busy on supper plates, he guessed.

"Josh!" he called softly. "Caleb!"

Caleb's face whipped into view between the flaps. "Quick!" he snapped. "Inside!"

Next minute Henry was sitting in his usual place at Josh's side, the flaps had been drawn together again and all the threats of the night were safely shut outside—or seemed to be.

"You weren't followed?" asked Caleb.

"No," said Henry. "I'm sure I wasn't."

"Shouldn't have come," said Caleb sharply. "Play *safe*."

"I had to," said Henry. "I think I've seen the man again."

Josh and Caleb exchanged one of their secret glances.

"He had green eyes," said Henry then.

Neither Josh nor Caleb said anything. The silence was not a comfortable one. It hovered, like a cloud. It was Caleb who finally broke it.

"Night train, Josh," he said. Then, again, "Night train."

Chapter 10

"*T*he thing is," said Henry, "what *about* the green eyes?"

"What about 'em?" said Caleb.

"I mean, why do they have green eyes?" asked Henry. "What does it mean?"

"Why does anyone have green eyes?" said Caleb. "Jealous, o' course. Jealous o' do-as-you-pleasers. Only some folks' eyes is greener than others, and their eyes is green as grass."

"Like a cat's," agreed Henry. "As if they could see in the dark."

"They can," nodded Josh.

"See in the dark?" Henry, aghast, remembered his elaborate precautions on the way there—wasted, as it now seemed. And there was still the journey home.

"Moon's no more'n a bauble to Greeneyes," Josh told him. "Night's day to 'em."

Henry pictured how the bare canal road with its long shadowy stretches must look to a Greeneye at this very moment, and shuddered.

"Only good thing is," went on Josh, "that day's *night* to 'em."

Henry stared.

"You mean that they can't see in the daylight?"

"Oh, just about," said Josh. "But only the same as you and me can see at night."

"The more sun, the less they see," put in Caleb.

"That's why we look forward to the summer," said Josh. "That, and the lack o' drafts, of course. We like to get into a bit o' green when the summer comes, and leave the towns to winter. No fuss digging holes in the country. We put up in barns and haystacks and travel light."

He sounded wistful, and Henry realized that he had for the moment quite forgotten the danger threatening them.

"It's been a bad winter for Greeneyes this year," said Caleb glumly. "We've dodged 'em here and we've dodged 'em there, and just when the light nights is coming and we think we're clear of 'em— they're on to us."

"But who are they?" asked Henry. "They don't live Here, do they? I've never seen anyone with eyes so green before."

"Oh no," said Josh, "they don't live Here. Don't live There, either, for that matter, though they'd like to."

"Then where?" cried Henry.

Josh shrugged.

"That we don't know," he replied. "All we know

is that they want to get There. That's why they're forever hounding me and Caleb."

"It's the night train they're after," said Caleb.

"And if once they get the night train," said Josh, "we're finished. They'll be There in droves, and that'll be the end of us do-as-you-pleasers."

"How many are there, then?" asked Henry.

"That we don't know either," said Josh, "and don't wish to know. All we know is, if ever one catches up with Caleb and me, next thing you know they're *swarming*. That's why we got to take the night train. Tonight."

"Not that *that*'ll be easy," said Caleb. "We shall have to throw him off first."

"We're three to one," said Henry, hoping at least to sound brave.

"That ain't the point," Josh told him. "The point is, if he's *listening*."

"Listening?"

"For the whistle," said Josh patiently. "The one that fetches the night train. That's what they're after, I tell you. If once a Greeneye hears that, the night train's his for the whistling."

"You mean she'll come to anyone?" cried Henry. "Even to me?"

"If you knowed the whistle," said Caleb. "Which you don't. Nor shall."

"When me and Caleb goes out and starts packing barrows and filling in that hole, that pair of eyes'll be watching," said Josh. "We shan't see him, but he'll see us. That's where we're put in a quandary, see? If it was day, we could give him the dodge. But if it was day, there'd be no night train. See? It's tricky. It always is."

"There ain't even a bit o' moon to dazzle him," added Caleb.

They sat silent for a few moments. Henry was thinking of a pair of light-green eyes somewhere out there on the dark embankment, watching them.

"Listen!" cried Caleb suddenly.

The other two started. Henry strained his ears for the sound of footsteps.

"I don't hear nothing," said Josh at last.

"That's just it!" cried Caleb. "The six twenty-five from Lincoln, it's not been over. And where's the seven four Special from Farthington? Where's the trains got to?"

"There ain't been a train since I come back," said Josh slowly. "No, there ain't. Four o'clock, that would be. There ain't been a train for close on four hours, Caleb."

Caleb got up suddenly and darted out of the hut. In a few minutes he was back.

"Not so much as a whisper in them rails," he said flatly. "Dead and cold. You know what that means, Josh."

"Line closed," said Josh dully, staring at him. "Line temporary closed."

"Temporary!" half-shrieked Caleb. "At a time like this! We're done for this time, done for!"

"Now hold on, Caleb, hold on," said Josh steadily. "Take things easy. We got to think clear."

"Done for," moaned Caleb again.

"There was two lines into this place, remember," went on Josh. "We sized 'em up when we was first ticking. There's another line runs in lower down, remember?"

"That's right," put in Henry eagerly. "There are two lines. The other one goes quite near my house. I can hear the trains when I'm in bed."

Both of them were looking at him.

"Busy is it, near your place?" Josh asked. "Shops and such?"

"Oh no," said Henry. "We're right on the edge of town. There are only fields at the bottom of our garden. There's a dike, then fields. And the rail- way——" he broke off. "That's it!" he cried. "You can go there! Camp in the fields—they'll never find you there!"

Josh and Caleb were looking at each other now.

"Could," ventured Josh cautiously.

"*If* we could get there," said Caleb. "There's a hole to be filled in and barrows to wheel. That Greeneye'll be watching all night. Can't be done."

"We shan't go at night," said Josh. "We shall go tomorrow. First thing. We'll pack our things up in here, so there's only the hole for filling and barrows for loading. Greeneye'll give up the minute dawn cracks. He knows there'll be no night train the minute dawn's cracked."

"And I can get up early and come down here!" cried Henry. "I can give you a hand with the packing and then show you the way!"

They both looked hopefully at Caleb.

"This place'll be *swarming* with Greeneyes tomorrow," he growled. "They'll be traveling tonight —black as pitch it is for 'em. We shan't have just one to dodge. Swarms, there'll be."

"We shall have to hope it's a fine day, Caleb," said Josh. "We shall have to hope for a sun that'll come blazing out and make 'em blind as bats. If the sun shines, there can be a thousand Greeneyes and they won't spot us."

Caleb got up and went outside again.

"The stars are there," he admitted grudgingly. "Cloud's gone."

"There you are!" cried Josh. "What did I tell you? There'll be sun enough to brown a harvest tomorrow, you mark my words. Truth to tell, I shall be glad to get in among a few fields again."

"Plenty of hedges, is there?" asked Caleb anxiously.

"Plenty," Henry assured him. "It'll be perfect for you."

"And that line ain't closed, Caleb," Josh said. "We can whistle up a train tomorrow night and be gone if the fancy takes us."

"That's true," agreed Caleb, brightening.

"Not but what it wouldn't be a pity," said Josh. "When a place ticks like this one does, it's a pity to let it slip through your fingers."

"It'd be a bigger pity to let the night train slip through our fingers," remarked Caleb sourly. "When there's Greeneyes about, we're better off There."

Josh looked suddenly gleeful.

"Better to flummox 'em, though," he said. "Better to stay and flummox 'em. Us running means them winning, and that's happened times enough. Spoiled dozens of good ticks for us, they have. Let's stop, Caleb, and *us* win."

Caleb, a sudden light in his eye, banged his fist on the table.

"Let's," he cried. "*That*'s the game to play. We've foxed 'em before and got away—now we'll fox 'em and stay."

Henry watched them in pure enchantment.

"Now you'd best be off, young feller," said Josh with an abrupt change of mood. "There's work for me'n' Caleb and it'll be up early for you."

Henry hesitated, thinking of the long lonely walk down the embankment road.

"And don't you go worrying about that Greeneye," said Caleb with sudden kindness. "It's us he's watching, not you. He don't care two pins for you. It's the night train he's after, remember."

"Just you set off now and walk brisk," instructed Josh, opening the flaps of the hut. "Caleb and me'll watch you from here. And you get down here by first light, if you want to see things hum."

"I'll be here," promised Henry. "I'll set my alarm clock."

"And bring a mirror with you," said Caleb unexpectedly.

"A *mirror*?" said Henry.

"As big a one as you've got," said Caleb. "You'll see. Good night."

He gave Henry a little push to set him on his way, and next minute he was marching steadily up the deserted road, his gaze fixed straight ahead in case it should accidentally turn aside and encounter a pair of green fluorescent eyes.

Chapter 11

$\mathcal{H}$enry's sleep was so thickly punctuated by the long hooting calls of trains that it was surprising that the alarm clock managed to wake him. It did, though, and kneeling on his bed to open the curtains, he saw that dawn was already at what Josh would call "the absolute crack." A faint crack of light did in fact splinter the otherwise inky eastern sky, and as Henry watched, a nearby bird let out the first loud jubilant call of the day. By the time he was dressed and had carefully let himself out by the back door, the dawn chorus was in full, amazing song. He stole down the dark deserted streets and from every garden came such ear-splitting whistles and deafening song that he expected at any minute to see windows thrown open and heads peering out to see what the din was.

"I *sleep* through this every day," he thought with wonder.

He had never heard birdsong so echoing and clear. It was as if the darkness had its own edges, as if it were a *tunnel* with its own echoes. As the light

strengthened, so the birdsong blurred and softened. Below he could make out the shape of the town hall dome and rows of rooftops like cardboard cutouts. He stole by a complicated zigzag route to bypass the market square and approach the canal bridge from the far side, as he had the night before. And all the while the gaps in the sky were widening until when he finally turned on to the canal road, it was to find the sun itself there before him, spilling fire into the smooth, dark water. The starry sky of the night before had fulfilled its promise. There would be a sun to cover their retreat.

As he approached, Henry could hear the steady chink and scrape of shovels and could make out the rhythmically moving forms of Josh and Caleb under the first arch. As he reached them the last shovelfuls were being thrown on the trampled down, though there was still a small mound of earth and stone left on the pavement.

"It's every time the same!" he heard Caleb exclaim. "There's always more comes out of a hole than'll ever go back in. Stamp and trample how you will, there's always *bucketfuls* over!"

They paused in their trampling and stood gasping for breath. Then they saw Henry.

"Good morning, young feller," cried Josh. "Seen the sun?"

He waved an arm toward the steadily burning water.

"That'll put blinkers on 'em, and no mistake."

"*That* one's gone now, anyhow, for the time being," said Caleb. "Heard him creep off just before sunup. Now then, young feller, get a bucket and let's clear this. Two bucketfuls apiece, and the job's done."

"Where shall we put it?" asked Henry.

"In the water," said Caleb, with a jerk of the head. "A bit of good clean earth never hurt fishes, so far as I ever knew."

Six heavy splashes later the pavement was almost clear.

"Just enough left there for bedding the tree," said Josh with satisfaction. "Get the tree, Caleb."

Caleb nodded and went over to the barrows. He came back with a small tree, its roots tightly packed in earth and moss.

"You're going to plant a tree?" cried Henry.

"Always do," replied Josh. "You can't just peg off and leave raw earth on a pavement. That ain't fair, that's not. I like to see a tree here and there myself, and so do most. Flowering cherry this is. Pink."

He dug a small hole within the original one, and while Caleb held the tree upright, stamped and pressed the earth firm around it.

"Pass us them last two bucketfuls," he told Henry, "and that'll about finish it."

"Now the fence," said Caleb. He padded off to the barrow again and came back with what looked like a big bundle of sticks about three feet high. He laid it on the ground and unrolled it, and Henry saw that it was really a kind of paling, wooden staves held firmly together with wire. Josh and Caleb, with a hammer apiece, banged it firmly into the ground to form a protective girdle for the tree—exactly like the metal railings used around trees in the park. Then they all stood back to survey their handiwork.

"A right neat little tree," said Josh approvingly.

"Paid our rent, anyhows," said Caleb, and went back to the barrows.

"You certainly think of everything," said Henry, again overcome by the thoroughness of their schemes.

"Got to," said Josh briefly. "If you want to do-as-you-please, you got to take it serious, like anything else. And now let's get them barrows packed."

Inside the hut the cupboards had been turned into boxes again and were stacked up ready for loading. The brazier had been emptied, the bed folded, the knickknacks taken down from the walls. The whole scene had the depressing anonymous look of a hotel room on departure after a holiday. Josh and Caleb evidently felt it too. After all, it had been their home.

"Come on," said Caleb, "no sense standing about staring at it. It was a snug enough little place, but there's better round the corner."

They all fell to it, and half an hour later the boxes were stowed, the hut dismantled and folded and the barrows covered with the tarpaulins, roped down to make them fast. Now that the actual moment of departure had come, Henry felt suddenly nervous. It was he who had suggested the long, dangerous move to the other side of town. Josh and Caleb were relying on him. He looked at his watch. It was a quarter to eight.

"We shall have to hurry," he said. "Everyone'll be going to work soon. And school."

"We don't want any of them children seeing you, Josh," said Caleb.

"You go ahead, young feller," Josh told Henry. "Keep well ahead."

"Got the mirror?" asked Caleb.

Henry nodded.

"Got yours, Josh?"

Josh tapped one of his bulging pockets.

"If you see Greeneye," said Caleb, "or even *thinks* you see 'un—flash your mirror at him. Get the sun on the glass and go for his eyes. The minute you got him dazzled—run!"

Henry closed his fingers over the edges of the mirror in his coat pocket, turned and began walking fast up the embankment.

" 'Ere, steady!" he heard Caleb's voice floating after him. "We're not on wheels, you know."

Henry slackened his pace. They met no one on the embankment. In the market square only a hand-ful of people were about, walking briskly or waiting by the bus stops. Nobody looked at Henry. The sound of the barrow wheels rolling over the stones sounded as deafening to him now as the birdsong had sounded earlier. He could see curious glances

being directed at the two coming up behind him. But none of the glances came from green eyes.

Then they were out of the marketplace and going uphill. Henry, in sudden panic, realized that he could no longer hear the rattling of wheels. He whirled round. There they were, far below him, almost hidden by their barrows, so steep was the slope. He looked quickly about, and seeing no one, waited for them to catch up. They let down the handles of their barrows abruptly and Josh took out a handkerchief and wiped his face.

"We can't keep *this* up," he said.

"You better tell us the way and hop off," said Caleb. "It's gone eight now. Like an anthill this place'll be in ten minutes."

"Just tell us rough how to get there," said Josh. "We'll be all right. Caleb and me've got a nose for a railway. We'll find it."

"You just keep on up to the top of the hill," said Henry. "That's all, really. Once you're up there you can see the fields, and you'll see one or two bridges, as well. Make for the stream. I'll meet you by the stream."

"Go on, then," said Caleb. "Quick!"

Henry started off.

"And keep that mirror handy!" called Caleb after him.

A little higher up Henry, after a check that they were still following, forked left and wove his way homeward through the side streets. At every corner he turned and looked behind him. Oddly enough, the nearer he came to home, the more nervous he became.

At the very last turn before reaching his own road he turned and saw what he had been dreading. A tall, thin figure of a man was approaching. His hat was pulled well down over his face.

"To keep out the sun!" thought Henry, terrified.

His fingers found the smooth sides of the mirror.

He took it out, angled it swiftly to catch the sun, and blazed light straight into the face of the approaching stranger. Then he fled. Behind him he could hear yells and pictured the enraged Greeneye standing blind and helpless, cheated of his quarry. With a last spurt Henry reached his gate and rushed round to the back door, where he collided with his mother putting out the milk bottles.

"Henry!" she cried. "Where on earth have you been? You come inside this minute."

Thankfully, he did as he was told.

Chapter 12

*T*hat morning Henry had to go into town with his mother. He dared not argue—there had been enough trouble already about his early morning escapade. As they set off to the bus stop Henry was chafing with impatience. If only he had known for certain that Josh and Caleb had reached the stream safely, it would not have been so bad. Even if they were already there, they might have set up camp in entirely the wrong place—because the right place that Henry had in mind was so perfect in every way, besides not being far from his own house.

So many and serious were his problems that it was not until they were right in Mandover itself that Henry remembered the real danger. Without warning his mother broke away from his side and "Look out!" he heard her say. "You'll be under a bus!"

The man whose arm she was gripping turned clear green eyes toward her.

"Thank you," he mumbled. "I wasn't looking where I was going." Head bent, he carried on along the edge of the pavement.

"I'm sure that man was nearly blind," said Henry's mother. "Did you see his eyes?"

Henry had seen his eyes. The man was not only a Greeneye, but a different one. The other had been tall and thin, this one was much shorter and nearly bald. Caleb had been right. The Greeneyes had taken advantage of the moonless night to travel—in their hundreds, perhaps, or even in thousands. Mandover was probably swarming with them.

It was Henry's mother who noticed the next odd thing, too.

"Funny," she remarked, "what a lot of people there are about wearing sunglasses. It might be a nice day, but I'm sure it's not sunglasses weather yet."

They were in the square, and looking round, Henry spotted immediately six people wearing dark glasses. As he watched, one of them almost blundered into a bus stop, and put out a hand to prevent himself falling into the road. For a moment the innocent sunlit scene, with its familiar midmorning bustle, was bathed in the horror of nightmare. Mandover, all unaware, was invaded.

After that it was a relief to follow his mother into a shop to try on shoes, and an even greater relief when she suggested that they should go home.

"It's such a lovely day," she said, "it's a pity to waste it in town."

Henry saw his opening.

"Yes. You know what I think I'll do?" he said. "I think I'll take some food and go into the fields. I could go down to the stream."

"Would you really enjoy it, picnicking by your-
self?" she asked doubtfully.

"Oh yes, I would!" Henry assured her fervently.
"And there are some huge chestnuts there—I could
bring you some sticky buds back."

An hour later Henry ran over the plank that
served as a bridge over the dike and sped down
toward the stream, his feet jarring and thudding on
the uneven turf. It was not really far, perhaps half or
three-quarters of a mile, but the land was rolling, all
hillocks and little valleys and hawthorn thickets.
Henry could not actually see the stream until he

reached the top of a steep slope that formed one side of a kind of miniature ravine. This was Henry's own favorite place, the ideal spot that he had had in mind for Josh and Caleb.

Giant trunks of trees reared on either side, their roots exposed because of the steepness of the slope. Beautiful roots they were, gray and sculpted and somehow *bony*, clutching at the steep fall of clay. It was partly the patches of exposed clay that made the copse seem always colorful, on even the bleakest winter day. A bright copper girdle of leaves still circled the lower branches of the beech, down below the wind's reach. Lichen ran like green fire, an impossible, burning green, over fallen logs, sticks and stones. To Henry, who had seen it all a hundred times before, today the scene emerged only as a blur of rust and pewter. For there, lying on the far bank, toes turned up and hats tilted over their faces, were Josh and Caleb. The barrows were drawn up nearby and Henry could see signs of a meal—the stove had been set up and crockery was lying beside it. Above them, rooks were haggling, fighting rudely over twigs and straw for their great untidy nests.

Henry stared down at the sleeping pair, astonished, and yet at the same time delighted that his favorite place should have seemed perfect to them, too. With a subdued roar a train sped suddenly by—out of sight yet only a hundred yards or so away beyond the other side of the little ravine. Slowly Henry descended, careful not to slip on the clay, and reached the edge of the stream where fallen logs formed a rough bridge to the other side. He was just over when he heard Josh's voice.

"Hello, it's the young feller again! There, Caleb, what did I tell you?"

Caleb did not reply. The hat moved rhythmically up and down over his face.

"Wore out," explained Josh, lowering his voice. "Not a wink last night. Not a wink."

"I shouldn't think so," said Henry sympathetically, "with that Greeneye hanging around."

"Greeneye?" exclaimed Josh loudly. Then he remembered himself and went on in a stage whisper, "*He* didn't make no difference. There was no harm he could do us. It was them *trains*."

"Trains?" repeated Henry, puzzled. "But there *weren't* any trains."

"That's just it," said Josh.

Henry, with a sudden memory of the nagging, empty space left by a stopped clock, understood.

"Best let him sleep," Josh went on. "He'll drop into the glooms if he's woke. Dinner'll wait."

He sounded wistful.

"I've got some food," said Henry eagerly. "I've brought plenty."

Besides the sandwiches he had cut generous slices from all the cakes he could find, and the bottom of his rucksack was stuffed with fruit. He pulled everything out and laid it on a fallen log for Josh's inspection.

"I'll put the kettle on," decided Josh. He advanced

toward the gas stove and stood measuring it, studying the various knobs and valves.

"I've got some lemonade," offered Henry. An explosion would probably rouse every Greeneye in the district. It would certainly drop Caleb well and truly into the glooms.

Josh pulled his tarpaulin up to the fallen trunk, spread a rug, and they sat down companionably to their meal.

"I like a sandwich now and then myself," said Josh, cheeks bulging. "But it don't do for Caleb. Gravy for blood, he's got."

"He's certainly a good cook," agreed Henry. "Marvelous."

"He can no more let a saucepan alone than I can let a sheet of paper," Josh went on. "His head's *stuffed* with recipes. Lucky we got to eat three times a day, that's what I tell him."

They sat chewing at the suddenly dull and tasteless sandwiches. Henry, looking round at the familiar scene, tried to capture this moment, with Josh at his side tossing crusts for the birds and Caleb snoring peacefully under his hat. He wanted to remember it so that when afterward he came here alone and the world had shrunk back to its proper size, he could actually believe that once they had been there. The stream ran flecked with borrowed blue and the sun lit fire among the bright girdles of the beeches. Best of all was the wind, racing over the bent grasses and badgering the stiff boughs above them, sky high. The *wind*'s a do-as-you-pleaser, thought Henry.

"Daffodil weather," commented Josh, as if his thoughts had been following Henry's own. Then, musingly, "I wonder where *she* is?"

"The night train?" asked Henry.

Josh nodded.

"You won't call her, will you?" cried Henry. "Not tonight? You're safe here."

He looked round the lively sunlight of the clearing and there was none of the lurking menace of the blank canal road. But he remembered the Greeneyes in the market square and a threat went over him as if the sun had suddenly gone in.

"Seen any Greeneyes?" Josh asked.

"One followed me," admitted Henry. "I flashed my mirror and blinded him."

He pushed the memory away.

"There were some in Mandover this morning, wearing sunglasses."

"Ah!" Josh took another sandwich. At that very moment the sun went in. There was sudden cold and bleakness. At that moment, too, Caleb woke up. He was awake in an instant, his eyes blinking rapidly. He glared round him with something like panic.

"The trains!" he cried. "Where's the trains?"

"Now then, Caleb," said Josh soothingly. "There's a line just over the top and trains going neat as shuttles."

Caleb scrambled up, brushing at his clothes and muttering.

"Put the kettle on," suggested Josh.

Caleb stood staring at the two of them, his face pale and wild.

"I had a dream," he said. "Greeneyes. Trains."

"You would have," nodded Josh. "You just put the kettle on, Caleb."

Caleb did not budge.

"*You* believe in signs, Josh," he said slowly. "Now *I* got one. You follow your signs. I'm following mine."

They looked at him.

"Night train," he said.

This time, Henry knew, he meant it.

Chapter 13

Josh made no attempt to talk Caleb out of his decision. On the contrary, he was full of interest in Caleb's "sign" and anxious to give it all proper respect.

"Fancy *you* having a sign!" he exclaimed. "That *is* something! That means something, and no mistake."

"Green eyes burning in a circle like candles on a cake, I saw," said Caleb, making the most of it. "And the night train plummeting up through the dark, straight into the middle of 'em."

He shuddered, and Henry and Josh, thinking of it, shuddered with him.

"How would they find us, though?" asked Henry. "They were in Mandover this morning, I saw them."

"It ain't no use questioning," said Josh. "Signs is signs, and no questions asked."

"They could follow the line," said Caleb. "They know we've gone somewhere, and they know there was no night train. They don't let grass grow under their feet, Greeneyes. They're looking for us at this very minute."

The vaults of the trees creaked in warning. But the sun came out again and Josh, throwing out his arms, cried suddenly, "Let 'em look! We're snug enough here, ain't we? And come sunset we'll have that beauty here for the whistling. Come on, Caleb, the kettle's ready. It's a ride in the dark for us tonight, and who knows what in the morning?"

Josh was alight with the prospect of adventure. Henry, appalled by the prospect of a world without the night watchmen, was stirred despite himself by the thought of beckoning rails and night journeys into unseen distances.

"What's for dinner?" said Caleb. "It's past lunchtime now."

"We had sandwiches," said Josh apologetically. "Nice, they were—for what they were. There's some left for you."

Caleb stared gloomily at the half-empty paper bags and rows of apples.

"Lunch!" he said bitterly.

"There's no harm going without gravy now and then," Josh said. "I'll tell you what, Caleb. You eat some of them and get your strength, and then you can set about a proper banquet. You, me and the young feller. A farewell banquet."

Caleb's face lightened grudgingly.

"Depends what we've got," he said. "You can't make a banquet out of half a dozen eggs."

"*You* can, Caleb," said Josh. "You eat them sandwiches, then have a ferret round in the barrows."

Caleb shrugged and carried the teapot over to the tree trunk and sat for a full two minutes glaring at the sandwiches before taking one and biting into it.

"What time's sunset?" he asked through his first mouthful. Josh rummaged in his pocket and fetched out his diary.

"Sun sets seven eighteen," he read out. "That'll just give us nice time to get supper over. The banquet over," he amended hastily. "Say it takes her half an hour to get here. We'll start at half-past six, whistle her at seven eighteen and we shall just have time to wash up before she comes."

Henry thought rapidly.

"I'll *see* her, then!" he cried. "I'll actually see her!"

Caleb looked at him sternly.

"The minute your supper's ate, you'll bolt," he said.

Henry stared back at him.

"Now then, Caleb," put in Josh, "no harm in the lad stopping. Young fellers likes trains. It'll be someone to wave us off. We've never *had* a wave off, Caleb."

"If my sign's the sign I think it is," said Caleb, "that young feller ain't safe. *None* of us is safe. I tell you I see a ring of green eyes. I see green eyes in *utter hundreds*. There was doom clapping in my ears when I woke up. *Doom*. I don't want no more sandwiches. I ain't hungry."

Josh and Henry, who had not shared Caleb's vision of doom, were nonetheless impressed. Whatever it was that Caleb had foreseen, it was evidently enough to put him off his food, and that in itself was disturbing.

"He's right, young feller," said Josh apologetically. "You got to think of your own good. If we take off on the night train and this here spot's left full of Greeneyes, it won't be no place for you. They'll be ugly."

He gazed slowly about him and Henry imagined the dark and the wind and the shining battery of light green eyes, with acres of empty moonless turf between him and home. For a panic-stricken moment he almost decided not to come at all.

"As long as you're gone by sunset and get off at a good run, you're safe," Josh decided.

"When we *whistle*," said Caleb with emphasis, "he *got* to be gone."

Josh nodded slowly.

"Got to be," he agreed.

It was useless to argue. Henry's dreams of the night train with her silver smoke and shining lamps would have to remain dreams. He stared first at Josh, then at Caleb, wondering for the thousandth time if they were *real*, if he were not imagining the whole thing. The smooth silver of the trees reared about them. Bands of sunlight flooded the two night watchmen, picking out detail—the red-gold of Caleb's eyelashes to match his hair, red clay smeared at the bottom of Josh's long coat and curling up round the sides of his boots. Of one thing Henry felt certain. However hard he stared at them now, however carefully he hoarded their every word, by the time the week was out, or the month, or the year, he would not be able to believe in them. Their very existence would be impossible and they would be lost to him forever.

"Unless I could see the night train," he told himself. "If only I could see her. Then I'd *have* to believe in it."

"Where will you go next?" he heard himself say out loud.

Josh and Caleb exchanged glances.

"Where, Caleb?" asked Josh at last.

"*There*, I say," replied Caleb. "Have a bit of a rest. My nerves is in shreds."

"But I ain't got nothing to *write*," objected Josh. "Hardly a few pages this place'll make."

Caleb turned away and went over to the barrows.

"If there's going to be a banquet," they heard him say, "there'll have to be butter. No butter, no banquet."

Josh stood up, hitched his rope belt round his middle and made for the stream. Henry, after a moment's hesitation, followed him. Josh seemed so sunk in his own thoughts that conversation was pointless. Henry stood silent at his side, watching the water run over the pebbles, breaking reflection, shattering the sky. Josh snapped a twig from a bough and tossed it in. Henry watched it sail slowly downstream, waltzing and gliding out of sight.

"That's us," commented Josh briefly, and went back up the bank.

Caleb was still rummaging about in the barrows

and a line of cooking utensils was ranged up on the grass.

"We shall have to get a table set up, Josh," he said, seeing their approach. "And there's my scales buried down here somewhere. They'll have to be got out."

The banquet was evidently on. Josh turned and gave Henry a slow wink before joining Caleb to set about stacking up boxes for Caleb to work on. Soon the place began to look like home. Josh, straightening up at last and taking a long look round him, said:

"You're *sure* about that sign, now, Caleb? It ain't wore off?"

Henry held his breath. Caleb, soup ladle in hand, whirled round.

"All right, Caleb," said Josh hastily. "That's all right. I just asked, that's all."

Caleb gave him a long speechless glare, then turned back to the barrow.

"It ain't wore off," said Josh to Henry in a low voice. "*Must've* been a sign."

He himself returned to the barrows then, and a few minutes later triumphantly came up with a blue-backed exercise book.

"Got to make some notes," he told Henry.

He seated himself on a fallen log and was straightway lost, hunched over the page, laboriously writing, stopping sometimes to chew the end of his pencil but never for a moment looking up. Caleb had begun to measure his ingredients. Henry stood there at a loss.

All the while a plan was taking form in his mind.

It had been growing ever since the moment when Caleb had told him that he must go at sunset, before the night train was so much as whistled. Henry knew that for all the notice Josh and Caleb would take of him that afternoon, he might as well go home. But before he went, there was one thing he had to make absolutely sure of. He edged up to Josh until he stood at his shoulder, then coughed loudly. Above him the rooks, shouting their nonstop ruderies, mocked him from their rocking toeholds. Henry coughed again.

"Mr. Josh . . ." he managed at last.

Josh's head lifted slowly.

"I'm going now," Henry told him.

"Ah, well, that's it, young feller," said Josh vaguely.

"I'll be back for the banquet," Henry said. "Six thirty sharp. But Mr. Josh . . ."

"What?" asked Josh. Henry was close enough to see the color of his eyes, usually unimportant in view of the magnificence of his beard. They were gray, like smoke.

"You did say the Greeneyes were blinded by light?" said Henry.

"That's right," agreed Josh. "No need for you to worry, young feller. You'll be gone by sunset."

"*Really* blinded, though?" persisted Henry. "I mean, they absolutely can't see?"

Josh surveyed him.

"The more light, the less they see," he said. "The

more dark, the less *we* see. Same thing, but entirely opposite."

"Thank you," said Henry. "I'll see you later."

He edged over the log bridge, climbed the steep embankment opposite and looked back for a last glimpse of the night watchmen. It occurred to him, seeing them bent over their tasks, that all the Green-eyes in the world could steal up on them at that particular moment without their even noticing. The thought disturbed him briefly. He himself would be away for the whole afternoon, there would be no one to warn them.

But they looked so safe down there, so much a part of the landscape, that even the rooks behaved as if they were not there. They were camouflaged by their roughness and brownness, and as self-contained as stones. Henry turned away and left them.

There was organizing to do at home that afternoon, and things got off to a bad start.

"Mr. Seaton's been telling me about you," said his mother, almost as soon as he set foot in the house. "I don't know where you get your ideas from. Such a silly trick. You could have blinded him."

Henry stared at her.

"Now don't pretend you don't know what I'm talking about," she went on. "It's bad enough getting up at all hours and wandering off without a word to anyone, but when it comes to flashing mirrors in people's eyes, especially old people's——"

"Mr. Seaton?" stammered Henry. "Was it Mr. Seaton?"

He felt nothing so much as relief.

"Who did you think it was?" his mother demanded.

Henry mumbled what he hoped passed as a reply and escaped up the stairs.

"You go round and say you're sorry after tea. Do you hear me?" his mother called after him.

"Yes, all right," Henry called back. "I *am* sorry, anyway. It wasn't meant to be him."

In his own room he shut the door and stood on a chair and began to feel about on top of the wardrobe. Finally his fingers encountered what they were searching for—a large, bulging paper bag. He brought it carefully down and spent some time checking its contents. Then, satisfied, he put it into his rucksack.

He lay back on the bed for a while, thinking about the evening ahead, the banquet, the whistling up of the night train and, hovering about the edge of all his thoughts, the Greeneyes. He saw them in rings now, as they had been in Caleb's dream.

With a final grin at Mr. Seaton (who was an elderly neighbor who bred spaniels) having been mistaken for a Greeneye, he went down to tell his mother the story he had invented to account for his absence that evening. It was a good story, he reflected, but not half so good as the truth was going to be.

Chapter 14

*H*enry had had to conceal his rucksack behind a shrub near the front gate during the afternoon, and he collected it as he set off, just after six, for the farewell banquet. He ran for the first few hundred yards until he was safely out of sight of the house. He had worked out the detour he would have to make in order to avoid suspicion. It was an easy one, really, and simply meant going along three sides of a square. All he had to do was walk to the very end of his road, where a stile beyond the last house led into the fields. Once there he could make for the stream and retrace his steps along it till he reached the encampment.

Henry enjoyed the walk. A low pale flood of sunlight bathed the fields and the long shadows cast by the little hummocks mysteriously altered the whole landscape, making it mountainous, adventurous. The earth was beginning to smell of dew and the grass, that was half hay and half new green, shook under the fitful gusts. There was no one else in sight and the Greeneyes seemed so unreal, so impossible to imagine in this golden evening, that by the time he had reached the top of the ravine Henry had forgotten their very existence.

The night watchmen were still there. Henry stood watching them moving about their makeshift tables, needing, as usual, a few moments to accustom himself to the fact that they were there, unmistakably real now that once more they were in sight.

A gust of wind carrying the steam from Caleb's stove set Henry scrambling eagerly down the steep slope, using the toes of trees as footholds for his own toes, recovering his balance by the bank before venturing on the precarious catwalk over the stream.

Josh and Caleb had moved their belongings near to the bank of the stream, where the ground was more level and water was handy.

"Hello," said Henry. "It smells good."

Josh and Caleb looked up. "I was right," Henry thought. "A Greeneye could have crept up without their even knowing."

"When Caleb does a banquet, it *is* good," said Josh.

Caleb, after a brief nod to Henry, had gone back to stove duty, lifting lids, sniffing, stirring rapidly, putting lids on again.

"It'll be a downright pleasure," he observed during a temporary lull, "to get back There again, where I can lay my hands on some ingredients. This ain't my *best*." He turned on Henry. "I can do better than this. Don't go thinking this is my *best*, because it ain't."

He whipped back to the stove and opened the oven. Josh leaned confidentially toward Henry.

"Nerves," he whispered hoarsely. "Always gets like this just afore dishing up. Like a fox on a splinter."

A train went by, the roar blown over their heads, and Josh cocked his head, suddenly alert.

"There she goes, Caleb," he said. "All set? We got to keep to the timetable."

Josh and Henry drew up their boxes and waited while Caleb served.

"A proper banquet hall," observed Josh, looking round. Henry, looking with him at the smooth gray pillars of trees with their dark ivy garlands, and the live green carpet of moss, agreed.

Caleb's gravy kept them quiet for the first part of the meal. By the time the pot had been tipped upside down to catch the last rich drops, and knives and forks had been regretfully laid down, the light was fading fast. The rooks chuntered themselves into silence and only an occasional whistle rang out in the quiet. Henry, waiting for the dessert, found himself looking nervously behind him where the stream had turned to iron and the far bank was already swallowed in shadow.

It was lemon meringue again, and Caleb was evidently disgusted with himself. He banged the plates down in front of them.

"It ain't my fault," he muttered. "The things I

could've done. Apples Marguerite, I *would've* done, or Chocolate Pompadour. No apples, no chocolate, no this, no that."

"It's my favorite," Henry assured him, surprised to find that his voice came out as a hoarse whisper. "*Really*."

"Anyhow, you've got the *other* yet," said Josh, giving Caleb a dig.

Caleb shrugged, and they all took up their spoons. Looking back on it, it seemed to Henry to have been a disappointingly silent meal. He had known that this was his last hour with the night watchmen and had set out full of the things he would say to them, the questions he would ask. Yet, at the time, only silence seemed possible in that strange twilight setting, with tangerine-colored shreds of sky floating like lanterns above the bare branches, and the darkness striding in across the meadows.

"You got to shut your eyes now," Josh told Henry, as the plates and spoons were removed and Caleb went back to his work table. "Shut 'em till I say."

Henry shut his eyes. He heard scuffling, a few whispers, the sound of matches being scraped and then "Open!" commanded Josh.

Henry opened his eyes to see candles dancing, a ring of tiny flames spattering the dusk.

"It's a cake," said Josh unnecessarily.

Henry was staring at the train that was drawn on the top, with blue icing smoke curling from her funnel, and spoked wheels.

"Is that *her*?" he asked.

"For you to get a picture of her, d'ye see," explained Caleb. "Nearest I could get to her. Don't really do her justice."

"Spent half the afternoon fiddling with it," put in Josh. "Had the cake baked in a tin beforehand, o' course. You got to keep a fruit cake, ain't you, Caleb? Longer the better. Would've kept till Christmas, that would."

"It's beautiful," said Henry at last. He was suddenly distracted by the sight of their faces, close together, bent over the candles, and with the realization that this was the last time he would see them, a swirling eddy of wind came diving into the hollow and the candles went out.

"Best cut him a slice to take home, Caleb," came Josh's voice out of the suddenly intense dark. "Time to whistle."

"Here," said Caleb, thrusting the knife into Josh's hand. "You cut it. I'll get up over the top and to the line. I'll whistle her while you get started clearing up." He peered toward Henry. "Good-by, then, young feller. You get off now, and good luck to you."

Henry sat numbly, dazed by the suddenness of it all. In a moment, the banquet was over, the game finished and the serious business of escape had begun.

"Good-by!" he called, finding his voice just in time as Caleb's figure reached the top of the slope and for a moment was outlined against the sky, one arm raised in salute.

"Here." Josh passed a wedge of cake, wrapped in paper, and Henry pocketed it, hardly realizing that he was doing so.

"Best do as he says," said Josh. "Peg off while there's time. Seems quiet enough, but you can't tell. Not once the sun's set."

He had already begun to clear the plates on to a tray and a minute later was swishing them in the stream, bringing them up dripping wet and piling them back again.

"Let me help," whispered Henry. Josh shook his head.

"You get off. There's only the boxes to stack in the barrow. Caleb'll be back in a minute."

He went past Henry in the direction of the barrows and Henry heard the clatter of crockery as he stowed the tray. Now he was back, whipping up boxes, stacking them one inside the other, absorbed as if Henry had already gone. Slowly Henry stooped and raised his rucksack to his back. As things had turned out, he need not even have brought it. It was all over.

"Good-by, then, Mr. Josh," he said, as Josh came at last to a halt beside him, out of breath and wiping his fingers on his coat. "I hope you get There safely."

"We will, young feller," said Josh. "It's an easy road from Here to There once you're on a night train and the wheels turning. You've been a good help, you have, young feller, and we thank you for it, me and Caleb."

"Thank you," said Henry, at a loss for words.

"Here he is!" hissed Josh then. "Quick! Off! Good-by, young feller, and good luck!"

"Good-by!" whispered Henry. "Good-by!"

He swayed dangerously over the stream and clambered up the embankment in his haste to make a getaway before Caleb saw him and blamed Josh. At the top he fell pitchlong, feeling the wet grass cold on his bare hands and soaking through the knees of his trousers. He edged round and strained his eyes into the little ravine where he could hear low voices and make out the shadowy shapes of Josh and Caleb heaving their barrows up the long slope. A minute later they were gone.

Chapter 15

*A*s his breathing quieted, Henry became aware of the silence and the loneliness. Getting to his knees, he surveyed the way home. In the distance he could see the tiny lights that were the windows of houses on his street. It was as if he were at sea and a vast expanse of dark water lay between him and harbor. As he watched, it suddenly seemed to him that he was not alone. He felt a cold light shiver run along the back of his neck.

He fumbled in his rucksack and his hand found the cold, hard shape of his lamp. It was a powerful one with a three-hundred-foot beam that he often used from his bedroom window at nights. Still kneeling, but shifting his position so that he was screened by a low bush, he turned on the beam.

Steadily he swung it in a slow arc. It picked out nearby grasses, etching each individual blade and seed, and probed the thornbushes to find last year's nests. His heart thudded fast and hard. Suddenly he held the beam, catching a glimpse of white that might have been a face. With horror, he saw that it was. And then an arm was flung up across the pale oval and he heard a faint cry.

With a tremendous effort Henry stayed where he was and swung the beam on. Again it stopped. A white face, and was it the flash of green eyes, or—the beam swung on—another face, another.

Henry shut the beam off. He stuffed the lamp into his bag and next minute was slithering down the wet clay slopes, grazing the hard roots of trees and rolling the last few yards to pick himself up and make the lurching journey to the far bank. As he started up the slope he thanked heaven for the darkness and in the same instant remembered that for the Greeneyes dark was light, broad as noon.

He heaved himself over the cliff-like edge on to the flat turf of the field beyond.

"Josh!" he shouted. "Caleb!"

But the wind was blowing the wrong way and he swallowed his own words and heard them float past him over the ravine to his pursuers beyond, advancing in the wide ring of Caleb's dream, seeing through the darkness with their clear cats' eyes.

Now he could see the railway lines ahead, on a low embankment, and called again, "Josh! Caleb! Josh!"

And this time there was an answer, so near and yet invisible that he let out a final terrified yelp before stumbling right into the cold, tarpaulin embrace of Josh's barrow.

"Hello, it's the young feller," came Josh's voice,

and next minute Caleb was snapping round him too, crying, "What's up? What's up? The rails are singing, Josh, she's coming! The rails are singing!"

"Greeneyes!" gasped Henry, with what felt like his final breath. "Hundreds!" He waved an arm behind him.

For a minute no one spoke.

"We're done, then," said Josh. "She's whistled for and coming. The rails are singing. There's no stopping her now."

Henry was fumbling again with his rucksack and setting the contents out on the grass, almost calm again because he saw that everything rested on him now. As he worked he heard the humming of the rails and then the loud whistle of a train and a groan from Caleb. As he finished, the train was upon them, and he lifted his head to see her at last, just as Josh had described her, red fires lighting her smoke, enormous lamps, white and green. There was a scream of brakes, a grinding of wheels, and then silence. Henry struck a match and cupped it with his hand, touching it to the blue paper of the cone-shaped firework by his foot.

"Quick!" he cried. "Get the barrows up!"

He moved over to the next firework, and the next, and as he lit the fourth, the first one was alight in a great white blaze of light. He heard Josh's voice:

"That's it! *That*'s it!"

The next few minutes were a daze of matches

striking, shouts from Josh and Caleb and fainter ones from the baffled Greeneyes, and above all the hissing snorts of the waiting train, chafing to be off. Henry lit the last firework and stood up.

The Greeneyes were there. Beyond the barrier of light they cowered, arms flung across their eyes. Others ran and were swallowed into the darkness. Josh and Caleb were aboard, their faces lit by the red fires of the engine, and Henry saw that they were waving wildly to him to come.

"*Up* you come," said Josh as he reached them, and a pair of strong arms pulled him aboard. He felt the heat from the fire on his face and pale plumes of steam drifted past him into the dark. Caleb pulled at a lever and there was a great, sighing hiss.

As the wheels slowly began to turn Henry looked back and saw that the last firework was slowly changing colors, and in the final emerald glow he saw the enemy—green eyes, green faces, green hair, green everything. Josh saw it too.

"We've tied 'em up in green ribbon!" he cried triumphantly. "Bright green ribbon! Come up, my beauty! Ah, we're away!"

With a sudden powerful striding they *were* away, the ground below was being drawn away from under them, and Henry, coming to himself, realized that he was caught, bound for There along with Josh and Caleb. Panic seized him. He clutched at Josh's sleeve.

"What about me!" he shouted into the smoke and wind. "I can't go There!"

"You ain't!" Josh shouted back. "Steady her now, Caleb."

Caleb was crouched over an array of brass knobs, valves, levers—he was the driver just as he was the cook. Face and hair afire together now, he swooped on a lever, pulled it down, caught a knob with the other hand and pushed it in. Then another. Then another. It was as if he were playing an organ.

The train was slowing, her breath lightened, her song broke into separate syllables. As she drew to a halt Caleb turned.

"*That* was a getaway," he said. "And we're only a mile or two off where we started. Safe enough now."

Henry could see lights not far away and a familiar-shaped building against the sky.

"I think I know where I am," he said.

"Right, then, down," said Josh, and then Henry *was* down on the suddenly cold and slightly rocking earth, and once and for all now they were in their separate worlds. He looked up at them, lit by the moving light of the fire, and then Caleb pulled his lever and a screen of white steam came up between them and the train started.

As the mist cleared he saw Josh's face peering round the cabin, and a waving arm. Henry waved back, the train rounded a bend and he was confronted with the blank eyes of the tail lights. When they in turn vanished, he was left only with the faint singing of the rails. Then silence. They had gone.

Henry turned and began to walk toward the lights of the town. Within half an hour he was wearily turning into his own street, with its curtained windows and sodium lights. Within sight of his own house he remembered the cake, and his hand went to his pocket.

"I can keep it," he thought. "I can *prove* they were real."

His pocket was empty. He thought of the chase over the fields, the tumbling descent of the clay slopes by the stream. It had fallen out. He stood in the bleak, shadowless light and turned his pockets inside out. There was not even a crumb. The cake had been wrapped in paper.

"There's always the tree," he thought. "Pink, Josh said, pink cherry."

But the tree could have been planted by anyone. Trees were always being planted. In the end there was really only one thing of which he could be quite certain. That whenever he heard a train hooting in the night, whenever he saw a tunnel or a hole in the road, he would think of Josh and Caleb, and remember that once, at any rate, they had been as real to him as the fingers on his own hand. And whenever he ate chicken or lemon meringue pie, whenever he saw a tramp or a flight of pigeons or a copper beech —or a sunset, either, for that matter.